SOUTH ISLAND NURSE

When both the Senior Medical Registrar, Sandy
Legrady, and the new house physician, Ian Dugall,
vie for her attention, Staff Nurse Erica Ryall is
forced to juggle with their affections . . .

Books you will enjoy
in our Doctor–Nurse series

SURGEON'S CHALLENGE by Helen Upshall
ATTACHED TO DOCTOR MARCHMONT by Juliet Shore
DOCTORS IN CONFLICT by Sonia Deane
NURSE AT BARBAZON by Kathryn Blair
ANGELS IN RED by Lisa Cooper
EVEN DOCTORS WEEP by Anne Vinton
THE ICEBERG ROSE by Sarah Franklin
THE GEMEL RING by Betty Neels
HEARTACHE HOSPITAL by Lynne Collins
NURSE SMITH, COOK by Joyce Dingwell
SISTER IN CHARGE by Judith Worthy
MARRY ME, STRANGER by Anne Vinton
MAJOR MIKE by Hazel Fisher
CHILDREN'S NURSE by Kathryn Blair
ACCIDENT WARD by Clare Lavenham
HEAVEN IS GENTLE by Betty Neels
THE UNWILLING LOVE by Lucy Bowdler
NURSE AT SEA by Judith Worthy
ALL FOR CAROLINE by Sarah Franklin
THE SISTER AND THE SURGEON by Lynne Collins

SOUTH ISLAND NURSE

BY

BELINDA DELL

MILLS & BOON LIMITED
London · Sydney · Toronto

First published in Great Britain 1968
as 'Where the Rata Blossoms'
by Mills & Boon Limited,
15–16 Brook's Mews,
London W1A 1DR

This edition 1981

© Belinda Dell 1968

Australian copyright 1981
Philippine copyright 1981

ISBN 0 263 73641 5

Set in Monophoto Baskerville 10 on 12 pt.

*Made and printed in Great Britain by
Richard Clay (The Chaucer Press) Ltd.,
Bungay, Suffolk*

CHAPTER ONE

As she dressed for Sandy's party Erica enjoyed the usual helpful comments from Marion.

'Your slip's showing.'

'Not really?' She hitched at a shoulder-strap. 'That better?'

'Yes, but won't it creep down again during the evening?'

'Oh, Marion, do be quiet. You're making me nervous.'

'Why did you buy a blue dress? Does Bobby like blue?'

'No idea,' Erica replied. She leaned forward to tidy a strand of dark brown hair that was straying from its appointed place on her smooth crown.

'No idea? You've bought a new dress for the party and you've no idea whether your partner will like it?' Marion's plump face was scandalised under the nurse's cap she still wore, although they'd been off duty over an hour.

Erica laughed. 'Now let's be honest, Marion. We both know jolly well that Bobby Guest only asked me to go with him to his farewell party because his first choice can't go. Bobby wouldn't care if I went in an operating gown. Anyway, he's leaving the day after tomorrow, so it's a bit late to think of impressing him with a new dress. Even if I wanted to,' she added casually, hunting on her dressing-table for her eye-shadow.

'Then who's the new dress in aid of? Bobby's replacement? Or could it be—Sandy himself?'

Erica kept busy with her search for the eye-shadow, although in reality she had remembered where she'd put it. Head bent, she avoided Marion's curious eye.

The truth was, she had chosen this new dress because she thought the colour did something for her—accentuated the creamy smoothness of her skin, reflected depth into her eyes, and set off her fine, soft, sleekly dressed hair.

Erica Ryall was a pretty girl by any standards, but her good looks were apt to be lost behind her staff nurse's uniform. On her silky hair her cap seemed incongruous, and the tone of the uniform print dress—a quiet dove grey—did nothing for even the rosiest complexions.

But once off duty, a new Erica blossomed forth. Then, by preference, she went hatless, and unpinned the soft hair so that it hung free about her smooth cheeks. Glowing colours replaced the starched apron and neutral grey dress to draw attention to a neatly proportioned, lithe figure.

This evening she felt she had produced just the effect she was aiming at. Whether she was going to all this trouble for the new houseman or for Sandy Legrady, the Senior Medical Registrar who was their host, she preferred not to say. So many of the nurses at Reidmouth Hospital were fond of parading their admiration for Sandy: and because Erica was fastidious, and perhaps also because in her admiration there was a tinge of something more serious, she preferred to say little on the subject.

Marion wasn't easily put off, however. 'I hear Sandy's a marvellous dancer,' she sighed. 'See if you can get a dance with him, Erica. I'd be interested to know if he's as good as they say.'

Erica heaved a dramatic mock-sigh. Beneath it there was a note of real wistfulness. 'If only he would ask me,' she mourned. 'The other men are hopeless.'

'The trouble with doctors,' Marion remarked, 'is that they so seldom have time for life's little elegancies. Take

Sandy, for instance, he's always up to his neck in work of one kind or another.'

'Some people have a natural flair. If you've ever watched Sandy on the dance floor you'll have noticed he *enjoys* dancing—he doesn't regard it as a chore, as most men do.'

Luckily, before this song of praise could carry Erica rather further than she'd intended, a heavy hand rapped on the door. A nurse still in uniform put her head round. 'Erica, Bobby Guest arrived just as I was coming in, so I said I'd tell you he was waiting.'

'Thanks, Joanie, I'm just ready.' She slipped her arms into her coat.

Joanie came further in. 'Don't you look terrific!' she approved. 'A new dress, isn't it? It's all wasted on Bobby, of course. Maybe the chap with him will appreciate it a bit more, though. He looks a bright lad.'

'The chap with him?' Erica was looking for her bag. 'I didn't know he was bringing another man.'

'Neither did Bobby, I imagine. He looks a bit dazed. The new man seems to be in charge, from what I noticed.'

'Oh, it's what's-his-name—Dugall. Sandy told him to bring the new man if he arrived in time. What's he like?'

Joanie shrugged. Being in theatres, she wasn't as interested in the advent of a new house physician as Marion and Erica, who were on a big double medical ward.

'He looks all there, if you understand what I mean. Got that alert, straight-out-of-Otago-Medical-School look. A couple of weeks on the medical side will soon wear him down to normal.'

'But what's he *like*?' Marion persisted. 'Fat? Thin? Tall? Short?'

'Passably good-looking, which is more than can be said

7

for the man he's replacing. And a lot taller, too, thank goodness—I prefer tall men. Not that I shall see much of him. If he's going to break any hearts, it'll be yours.'

'He won't break *my* heart,' Marion said. 'Nor Erica's— she's saving it for Sandy to break.'

'Now Sandy,' Joanie said thoughtfully, 'there's a man who could have my heart to chop in pieces, if he wanted. Not that he would. Even if he was interested in women, which he isn't, he wouldn't go in for heart-breaking. Much too nice.'

'I wonder if he's ever been in love?' Erica said before she could stop herself.

'Sandy? Not him. As I said a minute ago, he's always up to his neck in work. Moreover, in all the time he's been at Reidmouth, which is—what?—going on four years now, I've never known him show any interest in any one girl.'

'Wait till he does,' said Joanie. 'Ooh, boy, that'll be the day! Won't we have something to talk about *then*?'

'You're a pair of old gossips,' Erica scolded, making for the door, and dodged the pillow Marion sent after her.

In the sitting room she found the two men awaiting her, Bobby Guest, the departing house physician, and Ian Dugall, his replacement. Perhaps it was because Bobby was leafing through a magazine that it was Ian who took the lead in introducing himself.

'Good evening,' he said enthusiastically, taking in her groomed elegance with approval. 'You're Erica, Bob tells me. I'm Ian Dugall. I don't know if the name's familiar? My father was the great Ian Dugall—the specialist.'

'Oh,' said Erica, a little confused at being expected to remember his father. 'Oh, yes, of course. Dugall— Dugall—I don't think I can quite—— And yet the name's familiar.'

'Oh yes, his name still lives on through his work. He died when I was a boy, unfortunately.'

Erica met Bobby Guest's glance as he made his way to the door, and telegraphed her embarrassment. Who was Ian Dugall's father, and what had he specialised in? But Bobby simply raised his eyebrows in helpless token of ignorance, and led the way out.

'I understand your career is just beginning, Ian?' she remarked. That was a safe enough gambit; she had heard this was his first post since leaving Otago, the first part of his hospital training.

'Yes, I'm looking forward to it. It's a good first step, working under Galland. Galland is a man whose name will always stand me in good stead—"I worked under Galland" is a recommendation in itself.'

'What're you hoping to be recommended for?' Bobby asked bluntly, opening the door of his old car for them.

'Well, one hopes to forge ahead, doesn't one?'

'Oh, does one? To Harley Street in London, for instance?'

'It's a good idea to keep your sights high, I always say.'

Bobby got into the driving seat and turned to flash a grin at Erica, who had taken her place in the back. 'You spoke more truly than you knew when you said his career was just beginning, Erica. This boy intends to go far.'

Erica turned the talk elsewhere. Something about the newcomer's outlook struck a discord. She could understand and sympathise with a young doctor's desire to do well in his profession. But he surely was aware that the rewards weren't entirely those of money and prestige? Surely a man hoping to be a *good* doctor ought to be motivated by something more?

'I hope you'll like Reidmouth,' she began. 'It's quite a busy suburb, but near enough Dunedin for city life. And of course we have boating and swimming in the bay. Do you swim?'

'Yes, but I'm more interested in learning how to handle a boat. It's always a social asset.'

'You must get Sandy to teach you. He has a sailing dinghy. In fact, he lives over a boathouse.'

'That doesn't sound very elegant.'

'It's where we're heading now,' Bobby said over his shoulder. 'The man we're talking about is Sandor Legrady, who'll be senior on your "firm" under Galland.'

'Oh? Well, I suppose a Senior Registrar is allowed his little idiosyncrasies, such as living over a boathouse.'

There was indulgence in his voice. 'Who does he think he is, acting superior about Sandy?' Erica asked herself indignantly, and made up her mind to keep out of the way of this new arrival for the rest of the evening.

When they drew up at Sandy's place, Ian made a grimace of surprised appreciation. 'This is better than I feared,' he admitted.

Sandy had started a fashion by taking over the top half of one of the frame buildings used for storing boats and their tackle, many of which belonged to small boat firms round Otago Harbour who keep boats for hire on Dunedin's waterfront. He had converted the upper part into a huge studio flat, from which a flight of white-painted wooden stairs led down to the boardwalk.

At the top of the stairs he waited to welcome them. Part of his popularity, which was enormous, sprang from this attention to the small politenesses of life. Everyone worked hard for Sandy Legrady, because he never _demanded_ obedience; he simply worked hard himself and expected others to do no less. With his professional ability, published work, and personal charm to enforce his claim, his chances of being a consultant soon were considered high. And typically, no one begrudged him this prospect. On the contrary, some of his fellow-doctors wondered whether it would be a good idea to remodel their own untidy lives on Sandy's busy, well-organised plan.

They might have asked themselves if Fate would allow even Sandy Legrady to run his life so smoothly. The girls on the nursing staff, on the other hand, had thought about this. 'Wait till he falls in love,' they said to each other. 'Love can play havoc with the best of plans!'

But it seemed that love would never play any part in Sandy's life. Since he came to New Zealand as a boy from his native Hungary, he had had to work very hard. To learn a new language, fit into a new educational system, win his way to university and a medical degree, he had had to concentrate all his energies on work.

His success had seemed to Erica complete. She hadn't even realised he was not of New Zealand birth when first she met him; she had taken his name, Legrady, to be some form of the Irish surname O'Grady. But she had noticed later that he sometimes had a look of loneliness among the talking, laughing, back-slapping New Zealanders on the staff. She understood how he felt. Since coming from England to nurse at Reidmouth Hospital, she too had had moments of feeling lost or overwhelmed. But she loved her new friends and their lovely land. She loved the high snow-capped mountains inland of the town of Dunedin; she loved the vast lakes and the green rolling landscape. The flowers were such a wonderful mixture of the familiar and the exotic—one moment she would see a field of buttercups, the next she would see the brilliant red blossoms of the rata tree in the Woodland Gardens.

At least for Erica there were a thousand remembrances of home in this part of the world. Dunedin was so like Edinburgh in its way of life that she had had no difficulty in fitting in. For Sandy, there must have been a thousand difficulties. She admired him all the more for his quiet courage in surmounting them and never mentioning them. He was accepted by his colleagues as a first-class physician and a 'good sort'. The occasional parties which he gave were always popular. Erica was looking forward to this evening.

Bobby Guest made the introductions. 'Our new resident,' he announced, 'Ian Dugall.'

'Ah yes. The son of the famous Ian Dugall?' Sandy said cordially.

Erica thought she saw a tiny spasm twitch at the muscles of Ian's mouth. It had almost the look of irritation. But then her attention was distracted by the look of amazement on Bobby Guest's face at the fact that Sandy actually knew something about 'the famous Ian Dugall'. She stifled a laugh as Bobby challenged, 'Bet you don't know what he was famous for!'

'For his work on infections carried by the sand fly, and tropical diseases in Polynesia,' Sandy returned promptly. 'If I answer the next question, do I get to go on the Treasure Trail?'

'I hear I'm to be on Galland's firm,' Ian said. 'You're his Registrar, I believe.'

'That's right.'

It was usual for a junior man at this point to express pleasure at the prospect of working with such of his colleagues as he'd met—to say he hoped they'd 'make a good team', or something of the sort. All Ian said, however, was, 'I'm glad it's Galland. He's a coming man.'

'He's a bad-tempered old slavedriver,' groaned Bobby. 'He's worked me to skin and bone. And that being the case, Sandy old man, what about some eats and drinks?'

'This way, you poor starving maid-of-all-work. Take

Ian with you and see he gets what he wants——'

'I doubt if he'll get that *here*,' Bobby put in in muttered irony.

Sandy grinned to himself and turned to Erica. Foolishly, she found herself in something of a flutter. Would he notice the new dress? Would the colour prove a lucky choice?

'Evening, Erica,' he said pleasantly. 'Glad you could come. Stick with Bobby and the new boy for a bit, will you? Strikes me Bobby's taken a dislike to him. Smooth him down for me.'

She was both pleased and disappointed. So often—day in, day out—they had this same sort of conversation; he was always good-mannered, always friendly, yet there was never any closer contact. In the wards it was the same. She sometimes thought it would be worth the uproar of flagrantly disobeying him, of cheeking him, of failing in her duty, just to make him notice her as a person. But of course she could never do it. What he asked was always fair and reasonable, like this request for her help with the rather bumptious newcomer.

It was something, just to have him smile at her and ask such a small favour. She smiled in reply and followed the others.

Bobby soon made his escape and abandoned her to the delights of conversation with Ian on her own. Idle curiosity brought other members of the medical staff over to make his acquaintance, but they soon drifted away again; and when they'd gone Ian wanted to know the importance of each in Reidmouth's social ladder, and which of them was likely to be promoted soon.

She summed him up as an alert, confident and ambitious young man. She doubted whether she could ever get to know him better than she did this evening, and she was certain she didn't want to.

Now and then she tried to catch Sandy's eye. Later, when dancing began, she was asked for every dance—but never by Sandy. It was unreasonable to expect it; he had a great many guests to look after.

On the whole she enjoyed herself, but when the evening was over she was nagged by the feeling of having wasted her time. This was the last occasion, she vowed, on which she would set out with the admitted intention of trying to attract Sandy. Because, after all, why should he think twice about her? She was pretty, she was intelligent, she was ready to welcome any advances he might make—but so were half the nurses at Reidmouth. No, no, it was time she came to her senses and realised that Sandor Legrady had no time for romance.

When Ian came on duty on the wards he proved a decided gain. He was more sure of himself than Bobby Guest had been. Bobby had started straight from medical school too, and had been so nervous the first few weeks on his own that he'd driven them all, nurses and patients alike, nearly mad.

But Ian had an air of supreme confidence; the patients took him at his own valuation and were convinced they were in good hands. To the staff, however, the impression wasn't quite so favourable.

'He might say please now and again,' grumbled Marion. 'If Sandy can bring himself to say it, why not the houseman? Who does he think he is, anyhow?'

'Goodness, don't you know?' Sally Goodrich, the junior on the ward, had a gift of mimicry, and she used it now. 'Ian Dugall—son of the famous Ian Dugall, star graduate of Otago Medical School, you know!'

'Oh, Goodrich, that's him to the life!' cried Marion, giggling.

' "I'm glad to be working under Galland",' Sally went on, thus encouraged. She had deepened her voice to Ian's cool, clipped tones and somehow brought something of his thin keenness to her own rounded cheeks. ' "Galland is a coming man, and of course so am I!" '

'Oh, you're marvellous, it's just the way he talks!' shrieked Marion. 'Oh, I wish you were on my ward, Goodrich—it would brighten things up no end. And we could do with some brightening after His Lordship's finished ordering us poor slaves about.'

' "My father—he was the famous Ian Dugall, you know—always used to say that nurses were the lowest form of life in the hospital services"——'

'That was Captain Bligh of the *Bounty* talking about midshipmen in the British Navy,' Erica said, rather coolly. 'And that's quite enough of that, Goodrich.'

But it was too late. 'May I share the joke?' asked a voice which was the reality of Sally's mimicry.

The nurses wheeled and were aghast to find Ian there. Marion and Sally covered up with a hasty apology and scuttled off. But it was clear to anyone that the joke had been against the man from whom they were now escaping.

'What was all that about?' he said to Erica, who as senior nurse on the women's ward had stayed in case he wanted her.

'Just some foolishness—Nurse Goodrich is always up to something.'

She could have sworn that a momentary flash of something in his very dark brown eyes was not anger or indignation, but a sense of hurt. Was it possible that his armour had been penetrated by a junior nurse making fun of him? She was afraid he would question her further, but he let it drop.

Strange to say, she found herself thinking of that moment more than once throughout the day. She was sure he had been hurt. And after all, who is to say what may be hiding behind a bumptious, over-confident manner?

She didn't mention any of this to the others. But when Goodrich tried to repeat her mimicry act, she put a stop to it. 'It's not right to make fun of him,' she said. 'He can't help being the son of a famous father.'

'No, Staff, but he could stop ramming it down our throats,' the younger girl replied pertly.

'Perhaps he gets it in first because in the past people have tended to say to him, "So you're the son of the famous Dr Dugall". As a matter of fact, that's what nearly everyone did say to him that first evening—including Sandy. If I were in his shoes, maybe I'd get it in first too—as a sort of defence.'

Sally Goodrich looked unconvinced. And it was clear that the new houseman was never going to be as popular as his predecessor. Most of the nurses were just waiting to see him taken down a peg or two.

It looked as if the time had come, the day that Mrs Colworth was admitted. Sent up from Casualty, Mrs Colworth had been found in a state of collapse in the long-distance bus station near Reidmouth Hospital in the early hours of the morning. Preliminary examination by the house physician failed to discover exactly what had caused her fainting fit. Certain symptoms seemed to indicate infective hepatitis, but people don't as a rule faint from that. Ian looked puzzled, and Nurse Goodrich looked as if she were enjoying his puzzlement.

Tests were being carried out to verify jaundice when Erica came on duty. Ian told her he would be back presently to learn the results.

'Silly woman,' he said crossly, nodding at the patient. 'If she hadn't carried on so hysterically we shouldn't have had to give her a sedative, and then she'd have been able to answer our questions by now.'

'Night Sister tells me the patient was upset at not being able to continue her journey.'

'Yes, she's on her way to take up a housekeeping post at Lake Wakatipu. Not if she's got jaundice, she won't.'

Erica couldn't help feeling that if she needed a job and saw it fading because of an unforeseen delay in Dunedin, she'd be a little hysterical herself, especially if she were a frail elderly widow. But she kept these opinions to herself. In the rush of work at the day's beginning, she had little time for more than an occasional glance at the sleeping woman.

It was a grey, damp morning. The fog which had been forming in the Harbour during the night had crept up towards the town at daybreak. Now it was wreathing in and out of the big light globes down the centre of the ward ceiling. The bright steel surfaces of the equipment had a film of damp on them. Even the polished floor of the ward seemed less bright.

Sally Goodrich was doing pulses. All of a sudden Erica found the probationer at her elbow, her face white and scared. 'Staff, I think Mrs Colworth's choking!'

'Choking?' Swiftly she closed the door of the drug cupboard and went to Mrs Colworth's bed.

Sally's description of the patient's condition wasn't exact. Mrs Colworth was not choking; there was no obstruction in her throat. But she was having the most terrifying difficulty in catching her breath. She was sitting up, her face strained and discoloured, gasping painfully. And then she would push out each breath with even more difficulty than in taking it in.

'Status asthmaticus,' Erica said to the junior. 'Fetch Dr Dugall.'

While she was waiting she did all she could to ease her patient into a more comfortable position, with pillows at her back. Now she understood the cause of the collapse at the bus station. The fog had been hanging around the Old Harbour all night. Stepping out of the warm interior of the long-distance bus to go for a cup of tea, Mrs Colworth had been an easy victim to the fog's cold grey dampness. Anxiety about her job, weariness from her journey, and perhaps the onset of virus hepatitis had predisposed her to an asthmatic attack. It was a pity she had been in such a hysterical state when she reached the hospital that she'd been unable to tell the Casualty Officer she was asthmatic.

Ian arrived, looking flustered and rather fine-drawn after a night in which admittances from Casualty had left him little sleep.

'She's having an asthmatic attack.' Erica led him to the bed, and as she did so, heard him mutter 'Asthma?' in a perplexed way.

A brief examination showed that she was indubitably right. He ordered adrenalin, and they both stood by to watch it take effect.

'She'd better be specialled for a bit,' he ordered.

'Yes, sir.' Sighing inwardly, she allotted the job to Nurse Goodrich and made a mental note to finish the pulses herself.

Ian went back to his abandoned and belated breakfast. He had scarcely gone out of the room when Mrs Colworth gave a gasp and struggled once more to sit up.

'Good heavens, she's having another attack!' Erica murmured to Sally. 'Quick, fetch back Dr Dugall before he reaches the stairs!'

The probationer sped out of the ward after him. Erica took Mrs Colworth's pulse. It was alarmingly rapid. Her breathing was much worse—worse than the first attack. It might be due to an increase of impurity in the air of the ward, for as the morning breeze blew through Dunedin it swirled the fog into pockets and one of these had now formed round Reidmouth Hospital.

When Ian came back he took one look, and alarm washed over his tired features. 'But she's only just had adrenalin,' he said. 'She can't have any more, not with that pulse.' He looked over his shoulder, almost as if he were expecting to see something. 'The oxygen set——?'

'It's in use for the emphysema——'

'Yes, and in any case the Collison inhaler is an adrenalin method and she can't have any more adrenalin——'

Erica was dismayed by the patient's state. The poor woman was in the most terrible distress, and what was worse, in terror. Much more of this and it was doubtful if her heart would stand it.

She looked expectantly at Ian.

Ian, for his part, couldn't disguise his misgiving. 'We'd better get Dr Legrady,' he said in a low voice.

Nurse Goodrich hurried off to the phone at a sign from Erica. She was back in a moment. 'He's in Casualty. They've got a cardiac case down there that Dr Quillan needed help with.'

'Did you say we needed him urgently?'

'Yes, Staff. But they told me to say we shouldn't expect him for a few minutes.'

That left it up to Ian. If his Registrar couldn't come, the houseman must cope. She couldn't understand why he was still hesitating. She was on the verge of speaking sharply—urging immediate action—when a movement of his hands caught her eye.

He thrust them into the pockets of his white jacket. But not before she'd seen that they were trembling.

Under pretence of looking at the patient's chart Erica studied Ian. Colour had drained out of his face. In his eyes was a desperate uncertainty.

Then all at once Erica understood. He simply didn't know what to do.

It wasn't difficult to account for. He had been working at high pressure for several days and last night, particularly, had been a bad one. It is taken for granted that the houseman will turn out of bed no matter how little sleep he has had for the past few nights. Ian was tired, he was taken by surprise, he was inexperienced no matter how his confident manner might announce the contrary. Now his mind had gone a complete blank.

As if that weren't enough, the witness of this humiliation was the little junior nurse who had been mimicking him in the ward. How quickly she would re-enact his uncertainty, his stupidity! It would be all over the hospital in no time.

The junior's eyes were on him. There was something very like ironic amusement in her face. No doubt she was looking forward to Sandy's reaction when he came hurrying up from Casualty to deal with this emergency his houseman couldn't handle.

It was a distressing situation. The first consideration must be the patient, and Erica knew what ought to be done to alleviate her misery. Yet if she told Ian what to do, that was merely showing up his failure.

She glanced at him once more. He was staring at Mrs Colworth with tortured eyes. He wanted to help her. But the knowledge that should have told him what to do had for the moment been blanked out of his brain.

Erica herself had known moments of crisis when for a second or two a blackout took the place of all her experience. She felt renewed pity for the man at her side whom, until this moment, she'd always thought of as much too sure of himself.

'I can understand your hesitation, Doctor,' she began tactfully, aware that Sally Goodrich would report it all to her friends in due course. 'In the dark as we are about her medical history, there's no knowing if she's allergic . . . And then there's the possibility of jaundice . . . But if the aminophylline is given now, we'll know by the time Dr Legrady gets here——'

'Intravenous aminophylline!' Ian broke in, grasping at the name he'd been groping for. 'Quick, one c.c.——'

The effect of the drug was dramatic. Within minutes the frightful battle to breathe and exhale was over; Mrs Colworth lay back, and though exhausted she was safe.

'Shall I cancel the urgent call to Dr Legrady?' Erica inquired with a little smile.

'I don't know—perhaps he ought to see—— No, she's all right. Bring the oxygen apparatus up just in case, but you can cancel the call for Dr Legrady, Staff Nurse.'

But as they moved to the telephone the ward doors opened and Sandy came through. 'Well, where's the fire?' he inquired.

'It was Mrs Colworth, sir.' Erica met him and conducted him to the bed.

'I admitted her last night,' Ian said. 'Suspected case of hepatitis. It turns out she's also an asthmatic. Had the dickens of an attack.'

Sandy listened attentively to his account, his eyes moving from the patient to the younger doctor, with almost equal interest for both. 'So-o,' he said. 'Now we know why she collapsed. An odd little mystery neatly cleared up. You'll earn yourself another pat on the back from Galland for this, Ian.'

Ian bit at his knuckles. 'All right if I go and finish breakfast?' he said in a curiously flat voice.

'Yes, that's right, and if you're quick you can button-hole Galland as he arrives.'

'Yes,' he agreed, still in that odd monotone, 'another triumph to report.' He went off, briskly enough but with a stiff, tired tread.

'What's the matter with *him*?' Sandy asked.

'He's tired, I think.'

'Who isn't?' He cast a questioning glance at her. 'What's been going on here?'

'Nothing, really. He got a bit of a scare over Mrs Colworth, that's all.'

'Scared? The son of the famous Dr Dugall?'

'Even the son of a famous father's got to go through the mill like everyone else.'

'But being the son of a famous father does help to make the passage through the mill a bit smoother. Ah well, good luck to him,' said Sandy, but without great enthusiasm.

When he had gone Erica went back to her disrupted routine. Noticing that some of the breakfast things were still standing on a trolley outside the ward door, she went out to have them cleared. Someone moved in the ward kitchen. She walked a step further up the corridor simply out of curiosity, to see who was there.

Ian was sitting on the hard kitchen chair, his head in his hands. At the sound of her step he straightened and took some papers from his pocket, pretending to read. Erica's instinct was to walk away. But what was the good of that? She'd seen him and he knew it. Besides, you didn't walk away from a man in that state.

She went into the kitchen. 'Is anything wrong, Ian?'

'No, thanks—nothing.'

'You're not feeling under the weather?'

'No, why should I be?' Then suddenly he got up. 'Except that I nearly made a fool of myself a few minutes ago. It was you who saved that poor woman from suffocating, not me. You knew I'd gone blank, didn't you?'

'I—well——'

'It's all right, it's no use pretending.'

'These things happen, Ian.'

'But not to my father's son,' he said bitterly.

'What did you say?'

'I said the son of the great Dr Ian Dugall mustn't have a momentary blackout or do anything foolish. According to the family tradition, it just isn't done.'

'We all have moments like that——'

'But I'm not allowed to. It makes it just that much harder. Especially when I don't think I'd ever make it in any case——'

'Make it? What do you mean?'

'I'll never make a doctor.'

'Oh, Ian, you're reading too much into it. Even experienced men like Sandy can be at a loss.'

'But not over a simple thing like how to end an asthmatic attack. I knew one day I'd make a fool of myself. It's what I'm afraid of all the time. And when I do, it's going to be such a resounding failure, isn't it? The son of Dr Ian Dugall——!'

'Don't you think,' she suggested gently, 'that you worry too much about your father?'

He smiled faintly. 'Have you ever gone into a roomful of people and told them your name? What happens? They say "How do you do", don't they? To me they say, "The son of *the* Dr Dugall?" Every student at Med. School had his eye on me—Ian Dugall's son, the boy most likely to succeed! I've got to carry on where my father left off—everyone expects it of me, my mother most of all. Yet the more I try, the more I realise it's just a gigantic, disastrous mistake, I should never have been a doctor.'

'Now that's nonsense. Just because you were momentarily at a loss——'

'I'm always at a loss,' he cut in. 'If I didn't carry the books up here——' he touched his forehead—'I'd never know what to do. A real doctor develops a sort of sixth sense—an instinct. And they care so tremendously about what they're doing. I watch Sandy sometimes—and I just don't understand what drives him. He doesn't do it for the money, or to earn old Galland's approval—he'd slave away at it just the same if he were alone with a tribe of savages in the desert.'

She nodded. 'I think he would.'

'I don't understand it. Once I used to have some sort of inkling what it was all about, but—I don't know—I seem to have lost it in the continual struggle to keep ahead.'

'But need you be so anxious about keeping ahead, Ian?'

'It's my career, isn't it? The thing I'm trained for? I've got to live up to my father's reputation. But I can only do it by knowing the textbooks back to front and letting everybody know when I've done something clever. The way to the top for me is by sheer manoeuvring. I'm not like Sandy. I'm not a born doctor.'

She went up to him and laid a hand on his arm. 'You're just having a reaction after what happened. I've heard other first-year housemen talk like this.'

'But don't you see, they could afford to make mistakes? They could even be second-rate doctors if that was all they were capable of. But Mother expects me to be "worthy of the family tradition". I can't fail, I can't make mistakes. You don't know what it's like to be born into a family with a strong Scottish conscience.' He shivered. 'Oh, why didn't I have the courage to get out when I discovered it was the wrong work for me?'

'Ian—my poor man——'

'Don't be sorry for me. I've brought all this on myself. I was too much of a coward to fight against my mother's plans for me.'

'But it isn't too late to—— And besides, I'm sure you're wrong about your own capabilities. You'll find your sense of vocation again one day when you're least expecting it. I'm sure you will.'

He shook his head. 'It's sweet of you to say so. I've tried to tell myself that, but it's years now—over three years—since I felt that sense of rightness in what I was doing. I lost it while I was still a student.'

'It'll come back if only you'll stop being so anxious about what people think. I mean, if you could just forget what your mother expects from you, and work at the job for its own sake——'

'But nobody'll let me! Whenever I begin to think things are coming right, somebody happens along to remind me who I am and how I must be worthy of the name. Why else do you think I keep boring people with reminders that my father was a fine doctor? It's to make up for my own shortcomings. I'm sheltering behind his achievements. But I know other people think I'm conceited and silly.'

'No, they don't——'

'Oh yes, they do. Do you think I didn't hear that little cheeky nurse taking me off the other day? I know I sound cocksure—the one-hundred-per-cent career man, that's me. Do you know what they call me when they think I

25

can't hear? King Dugall the Second.'

'Oh, Ian, they don't mean anything.'

'I read somewhere that if you want to know what people think of a man, you should find out what nickname they've given him. That's mine—the name for a man who's no good on his own and has to trade on his father's reputation.'

'Don't talk like that. It's not true.'

'But it is,' he insisted sadly. Then, studying her earnest face, he managed a sketchy smile. 'Don't look so upset. I'm a fool to babble on like this to you. After all, what difference does it make to you?'

'It does make a difference, though.'

'Why should it?'

'How do I know? I can only tell you that now I know a bit more about you, I—I——'

'You what? Feel sorry for me?'

'Would that be so bad?' she countered, meeting his eye.

For a moment she thought his habitual cloak of over-confidence was about to enfold him again. Then he looked down at his feet. 'I've never spoken like this to anyone before,' he murmured. 'I really don't know why I had to tell it all to you.'

'Perhaps it's because I happened to see you for a moment as you really are—not Ian Dugall's son, but someone with a right to his own life and his own experiences.'

'It's a great temptation,' he admitted. 'To think there might be someone with whom I needn't pretend, I mean.'

'You needn't pretend with the rest of us. No one would hold it against you that you started off on the wrong foot.'

'My father really was a great man,' he said suddenly. 'It's not his fault his son's a washout.'

'But you're not, you're not——!'

'Well, I think I am. No good at the job, can't make friends or get on with people——'

'You're getting on all right with me, aren't you?'

'But that's different. You're ready to make allowances. Suppose I was to go out of this room now and say to people, "Don't think of me as Dr Dugall's son, think of me as a person"—what have I got to offer them? Oh, if only I could run away and start again, start on a new life that would be all my own!'

'Why can't you? Start again, I mean. Dr Legrady did it, you know. If you really feel convinced you don't want to stay in medicine——'

'Try something else. And live with the realisation that I'd wrecked Mother's hopes and dreams? After all the sacrifices she's made to send me to Otago? No, it's impossible. I'll just have to struggle along as best I can.'

'At least,' Erica suggested, 'you know now you've got someone with whom you can discuss things.'

'Would you——?' His face lit up. 'You wouldn't mind? It would mean such a lot to me. I've never really had anyone—not anyone you could really describe as a friend.'

'Then that's how you can describe me.' She held out her hand and he pressed it firmly.

As footsteps sounded in the corridor they broke away. Sandy paused on the threshold, surprised at what he'd interrupted.

'I thought you needed your breakfast?' he remarked to Ian.

'I'm—I'm just going.' Ian hurried out.

Sandy watched him go. 'Our Dr Dugall isn't his usual confident self this morning,' he commented.

'Even the most confident people have problems.'

27

'Everybody has problems,' he agreed. 'What are Ian's?'

'What makes you ask?'

'I don't know,' he said, surprised. 'Idle curiosity, I suppose.'

'Then it'll have to go unsatisfied, I'm afraid.'

'Aha! Secrets, eh?'

'It isn't anything to make fun of,' she said, with a tinge of indignation.

'No, I see it isn't,' he said, studying her with interest. 'You're quite annoyed with me for daring to think so, aren't you?'

'I'm sorry. I know most people think Ian's a good target for poking fun at.'

'But you don't?'

'Don't you understand that even a man most people envy can have troubles, and need help?'

'And you're offering yours?'

'Yes, why not?'

'Why not?' He thought about it. 'There's no reason, except that I think you've taken on a thankless task.'

'I'm the best judge of that.'

He leaned against the doorpost. 'Well, well,' he said thoughtfully. 'Who would have thought a quiet girl like you would have the courage to reject everybody's opinion of Ian Dugall, and back her own judgment? Erica Ryall, there's a lot more in you than meets the eye!'

CHAPTER TWO

WHEN Dr Galland made his rounds later, Erica was pleased to see that Ian was himself again. In fact, so much himself that he was showing off a bit about diagnosing Mrs Colworth. Once she caught his eye; he coloured a little, and she smiled to let him know she understood, and that her promise of friendship still held good.

He dropped behind when his seniors left the ward. 'Are you free this evening?'

She'd been going to write letters home, but dropped the idea. 'Quite free.'

'Can I take you up on that offer?'

'I hoped you would.'

'I don't know the harbour area very well. Do you know some place we could go?'

She knew just the place, a nice little restaurant up towards Blanket Bay. 'We could go to the Vista. It's not so close to the hospital that we'll meet a lot of staff.'

'Shall I pick you up at the nurses' home?'

She hesitated. If he did that, their date would be a topic of conversation within the hour. She wasn't *ashamed* of going out with Ian, but she dreaded having to face Marion's questions when she got back. She'd like to have a chance to know him better before she had to defend him to her friends.

'It would be better to meet outside Harbour Gate, since we're going that way.'

He accepted the suggestion with a readiness that made her ashamed. 'Seven?'

'I'll be there.'

Off and on, throughout the day, she thought about the evening to come. She'd better wear sensible shoes, in case they walked all the way there and back. That was a nuisance, because the suit she meant to wear looked better with court shoes.

'What does it matter what I wear?' she wondered suddenly, and coloured at her own silliness. A man asked her to listen to his troubles, and all she could think about was her own appearance. Why bother? She didn't want to impress Ian.

Now if it had been Sandy. . . .

She gave herself up to the pleasure of imagining a date with Sandy. Suppose he asked her out, it would depend where they were going—sailing, a country walk, or to a concert; these, she knew, were Sandy's chief interests outside the hospital.

'You're in quite a day-dream, aren't you?' Sandy's voice said.

Startled, she looked up from the ward linen-list. 'Why— I'm sorry—did you want something?'

'Only to speak to you. I tried to catch you this morning, but Galland dragged me off. Doing anything this evening?'

Erica's heart gave a tremendous jolt. She felt herself colouring foolishly.

'This—this evening?' she stammered.

'That cruiser I hire from Swanson's—it'll soon be too late for much more pleasure-boating. I'm taking out a crowd tonight, before I turn her over to the owners. Your friend Marion's coming, and Tom Quillan, and that new nurse in Orthopaedics—one or two others. Just a run up the coast. Like to come?'

'I'm sorry, Sandy, I'm afraid I can't.'

Disappointed, he said, 'Marion told me you'd no arrangement for this evening.'

'Neither I had, earlier on. But I have a date now.'

'In that case . . . Some other time?'

'Thanks, I'd love to.'

'I'll hold you to that.' He seemed on the verge of saying something more, but instead smiled, nodded, and moved on down the ward. Erica was left almost rubbing her eyes in amazement.

That he should have invited her——! It was true he often took a party out in the cabin cruiser, but people rather queued up for the chance. And since she'd been a guest at his place only recently, she certainly didn't expect him to include her in the outing tonight.

If only she hadn't already made a date with Ian——! Vexation darkened the clear blue eyes, and she couldn't help feeling something that was almost resentment at this trick of fate.

A trace of this feeling lingered in her greeting to Ian when he eventually came out of Harbour Gate.

'So there you are at last!'

'Am I so very late? I'm awfully sorry, Erica. Hamilton's covering for me and he took a while over his meal.' Hamilton was the other houseman on Galland's firm, an older man than Ian.

'It's all right,' she said hastily, ashamed of herself. 'I've just arrived myself, really.'

'Which way do we go? Are we catching a bus?'

'I thought we'd walk, Ian. It's rather pleasant along below Signal Hill on a March evening.'

He fell into step beside her. 'You know your way around the place pretty well, I take it. How long have you been out from England?'

'About a year and a half. It's my second job since I

arrived. I like it better than the first one, though the work's harder, since it's a new hospital.'

'How do you like it "down-under"? Is it all very different from home?'

'Goodness, no! I'm from Edinburgh, you know—and half the population of Dunedin seem to have come from there originally!'

'My people were from Skye originally, so Mother tells me.'

'Oh, I know Skye! I've climbed there with one of my brothers.'

'*One* of your brothers? How many have you got?'

'Two brothers, two sisters.'

'You must miss them?'

'I did when I first left home, but I soon got over it. I'm "happy in my work", as the saying goes. One of my special interests is therapy for long-term patients. That's what brought me to Reidmouth, actually. I read some articles by Sandy, about schemes for helping patients who'd had lengthy illnesses——'

'He's full of ideas,' Ian said rather enviously. 'You've only to hear him talk to know he has a brilliant mind. If he plays his cards right he'll end up with a knighthood.'

'A knighthood?' She gave a little surprised laugh. 'I bet such an idea never entered his head.'

'But he's ambitious? He's applying for promotion, isn't he?'

'Well, yes. But I don't think he wants it so much for the glory or anything like that. It's the wider opportunities—the chance to pursue his ideas.'

He said, rather enviously, 'You think a lot of Sandy.'

'We all do.'

'He's lucky. The right man in the right job. He even

has time and energy left to cultivate his friends. He's taken out a whole gang from the hospital in that hired boat thing.'

'Yes, I—I heard about it.'

'I hope they're all good sailors,' he said with a sudden boyish grin. 'That breeze from the Pacific Ocean is making the water quite choppy!'

He buttoned up his tweed jacket against the onslaught of the rising wind. Erica noticed the jacket was impeccably cut and of excellent cloth, though it was no longer new. She recalled that all his clothes were like that, hinting at a mind guiding his choice, a mind that looked to the future and, at some extra cost, selected what would always be a credit to the wearer.

The Vista Café stood on a little slope below Signal Hill facing west. A magnificent sea-scape of grey waters reflecting the setting sun justified the choice of name. Inside it was comfortable, without too many anchors and lobster pots to insist on its waterfront character. Thinking of Ian's pocket—for in her experience housemen were always hard up—Erica chose coffee and biscuits. Ian, admitting he had skimped his meal to be on time to meet her, ordered sandwiches.

'I don't know what Mother would say if she could see me now,' he confessed as he munched. 'She says you should either eat a proper meal, or not eat at all.'

'Theoretically, I agree with her,' Erica smiled. 'But this is nice, isn't it?' Her eyes grew thoughtful. 'What's your mother like, Ian?'

'Oh, she's a wonderful person!' he cried. 'Everybody admires her. She's an actress, you know—not famous or anything, but I think she's better-looking than a lot of faces you see on the posters.' He took out his pocket-book and extracted a photograph. 'There she is—see for your-self.'

It wasn't, as Erica expected, a snapshot; it was a quar-ter-plate version of a studio colour portrait. The woman who smiled out at her was in her mid-forties, with the kind of looks that can never be spoiled by the passage of time. Her ash-grey hair was beautifully groomed, her skin almost unwrinkled.

If there was a flaw, it was the hint of determination behind her smile. Here was a woman who made a plan and kept to it. Here was the woman, perhaps, who had launched her son on his career at some sacrifice, who had chosen his clothes for him and begrudged him nothing—so long as he accepted her opinions as sacrosanct.

'She really is very beautiful,' she agreed, studying the picture. 'Is she in films or on the stage?'

'Oh—well, she *was* on the stage. That was how she met my father—she was on tour in Honolulu while he was there. She gave it all up to marry him. She absolutely worshipped him, Erica. I can't describe what it did to her when he died. I was only eleven at the time, but I re-member how everything changed—like a lamp going out. Well, after a bit we got terribly short of money. My father was terribly impractical, you know. If he had money he spent it—chiefly on giving Mother marvellous surprises. He didn't even have proper insurance. So Mother went back to acting. But you know how times are hard in the theatre in New Zealand.'

'I've read about it—not much of a film industry to help out, is there?'

'Mother took modelling jobs to help out. She's even been "Mum" in one or two TV commercials. But it's pretty precarious and such gruelling hard work. When she gets a small part in a film, for instance, she sometimes

34

has to be up at five in the morning. So you see, that's why I've got to make good in my career. I owe it to her, Erica.'

Erica sighed. 'You mean so that you can give her an easier life? It'll be a long while before you can do that—unless you go into general practice, and even then——'

'No, I can't be a G.P. I've got to be a specialist. I reckon that if I work hard and miss none of the chances, I might be a consultant in my early thirties——'

'But you can't go into medicine as if it were an industrial undertaking with a post as managing director in the future——'

He nodded vehemently. 'I've met more than one chap who's done just that. Erica, admit it—lots of fellows come into medicine simply because their fathers are doctors and will take them into partnership later. They've no particular feeling about doctoring—it's just a way of earning a living.'

'Yes, but they're the ones who don't get the real satisfaction that's part of the real reward. The truly devoted man has something inside him that makes him work harder, struggle farther——'

'You're talking like a starry-eyed idealist,' he interrupted. 'Are you telling me that every consultant got there by sheer hard work and ability? That none of them pulled strings?'

'Oh, well, I agree some of them have used influence. But the right way to reach the top is on your merits.'

'I haven't any,' he said bitterly. 'So I'll just have to rely on getting to know the right people and pulling strings.'

'But it's wrong—you'll harm yourself—warp your whole nature——!'

'That's a chance I must take. All I know is that my

mother has pinched and scraped to get me this far because she wanted my father's name to live again one day.'

'It's not fair to ask such a thing from a child!' she exclaimed hotly. 'She had no right——'

'But I wanted to! Don't you understand? I thought I had the same ability that my father had. I believed I could carry on where he left off. I was so *sure*——' He shook his head at the memory. 'And then I began to find that it didn't work out like that. That magic understanding of the patient's needs—I didn't have it. In fact, you'll probably be shocked to learn that I thought some of them terrible bores, and a lot of the instruction was mere drudgery.'

'It's the same in nursing, Ian. But by and by, when the training is over and you find your feet——'

She broke off. Her attention had been attracted by a group of people stepping ashore from a cabin cruiser against the quay a short distance off. The twilight made it difficult to distinguish them, but Erica was almost sure ... Yes, that was Marion leading the way! Next moment she saw Sandy's tall figure follow the others. They ascended the slope from the jetty to the road, their laughter drifting up on the wind.

And then to her dismay she saw them turn and make decidedly for the café. Next moment they came in at the door, their faces flushed from the sea air, their gay chatter causing heads to turn.

When they saw Erica, they stared in surprise.

'Why, Erica, fancy finding you——!'

Marion had been too busy preparing for her own evening to pay much attention to Erica's plans. All she knew was that Erica was 'going out'.

She led the way to Erica's table. 'So this is why you couldn't join us this evening,' Sandy said from his place

36

at the rear of the group. There was a tinge of perplexity in his tone.

Marion, tactless as always, burst out with what she was thinking. 'You mean,' she said in astonishment, 'you turned Sandy down just to keep a date with Ian Dugall?'

CHAPTER THREE

LATER that night, back in the Nurses' Home, Erica took Marion to task for that appalling remark. 'What on earth possessed you to blurt out a thing like that? It sounded terrible!'

'It just sort of came out, Erica. It was what I was thinking, you see. I mean, you know how often you've said you'd love a trip on the cabin cruiser—and anyhow I thought you disliked Ian Dugall?'

'I thought so too. But I was wrong.'

'What on earth changed your mind?'

'It's not worth going into. I can tell you this, though, Marion—he's not the thick-skinned show-off we took him for. In fact, he's not thick-skinned at all. Which is why he took me home so quickly after you said your piece.'

Marion flushed. 'You're really angry with me, aren't you?'

'We-ll . . . Perhaps it was my fault. I should have told you who I was going out with and then you wouldn't have been taken aback. But I wish it hadn't happened. Ian was really hurt. All the way home he scarcely said a word.'

By next day the news had got round the hospital that Erica and Ian had been out together. Erica could feel the eyes of the others upon them when they encountered each other in the ward, but Ian had retreated into his disguise of slick self-assurance. She was extremely sorry to see it happen and tried to get a word with him. But he resolutely gave her no opportunity.

Sandy came to her at the end of his ward round to say, including Ian in the words, 'I'm sorry you hurried away last night. We didn't frighten you off, did we?'

'I had to get back anyhow,' Ian said. 'David Hamilton was covering for me.'

'Life's hard on a houseman.' Sandy commented. 'I never have approved of this continuous-duty system. If ever you want an evening off, Dugall, I could probably——'

'I'm quite willing to fulfil my obligations,' Ian interrupted. 'I shouldn't like to gain the reputation of not being keen on my work.'

'No, of course not, but——'

'I read the hospital rules when I signed the contract. In any case, I knew what to expect. My mother told me how my father had to keep his nose to the grindstone. He was at St Gregory's, you know, and everyone knows what discipline is like there.'

'Yes, of course.' Erica could see that Sandy wanted to be spared any more talk about Ian's father. He turned politely to Erica. 'Perhaps it was just as well you didn't come on our trip last night. The sea got choppy and some of the passengers got a bit green.'

'So Marion told me. But like most landlubbers, I'm convinced I'd be a first-class sailor if I got the chance.'

'Oh, come on now—plenty of chances in a place like Reidmouth.'

'Plenty,' she agreed. 'But fifty-pence's worth of hired motor-boat isn't my idea of being a sailor.'

'You mean you'd really like to handle sail?'

'I've often thought I'd like to have a try.'

'Pity it's getting rather late in the year. I don't think it's fair on the patients, you see, for medical and nursing staff to get their hands chapped in cold sea water—leaves the way open for infection. But we still get some nice calm days in March and April. Would you like to go out in a sailing dinghy?'

'Why, I'd love to.'

'When's your day off?'

'The day after tomorrow.'

'I could get away in the afternoon. It's a date, then, if the weather's fine. Don't forget.'

When he had gone on his way, Ian said coolly, 'You haven't an inconvenient engagement to spoil things this time.'

'Oh, Ian——!' Erica caught at his sleeve as he made as if to follow his senior. 'Ian, I'm not responsible for what Marion said last night.'

'I didn't say you were.'

'But you're acting as if I were,' she accused.

He wavered. Some of the asperity left his face. 'Am I?' he murmured. 'Perhaps it's a bit silly to get in a huff with the only person who's been nice to me.'

'I enjoyed our talk last night, Ian. I really did.'

'It would be a bit much to ask you to repeat the process, though. My day off is today week. If I could get tickets for a show or something, would you like to go somewhere in the evening?'

'If that's what you'd like.'

'Don't forget—put it in your diary in case Sandy tries to claim you.'

'Oh, he won't do that. In fact, he won't really take me sailing on Thursday. Something will come up to prevent it.'

'Something will come up? What on earth do you mean?'

'Sandy never takes a girl out on her own—only in a group. I mean there's usually a whole gang from the hospital. It would have to mean he was really interested before he'd take a girl out alone in that little sailing dinghy. And he's not interested in me. He was just being polite.'

She really believed this. Miracles didn't happen, that was her view. Sandy had just been making conversation. When Thursday morning turned out foggy, she thought, 'This is the perfect excuse for him.' So she wasn't surprised when he rang just as she finished dressing.

'Have you noticed what a horrible day it is?' he inquired.

'Yes, indeed. We shan't be able to go sailing.'

'Hardly. But the weather forecast says "Brighter later". Let's see what it's like at midday, shall we?'

Erica felt her throat go dry. She took a firm grip of the receiver. 'You mean—you really want to take me sailing this afternoon?'

There was a slight pause. 'I thought that was the arrangement?' he said on a questioning note.

'Yes, but——' She swallowed. 'I didn't altogether take it seriously.'

'But why not?' As she furnished no explanation he went on with a faintly puzzled laugh, 'Don't tell me you've made other arrangements? You're not going out with Ian Dugall, by any chance?'

'No, of course not, Sandy.'

'*Have* you arranged anything?'

'No-o . . . I was just going to spend the morning shopping in Dunedin and have lunch at Cosimo's. It's what I generally do if I'm on my own.'

'Then shall we meet at Cosimo's? About one-fifteen?'

Scarcely believing it could be true, Erica murmured, 'That would be fine.'

She had provided him with an easy way out if he'd regretted his original invitation; but no, he'd gone out of his way to make sure their arrangement stood.

Why should he bother? It all seemed to date from the moment when she'd championed Ian. He'd said then that there was more to Erica than met the eye. Could it be that he was—interested in her?

She had quite a few commissions for patients in her ward—postal orders to buy, books to order, and then she decided on the spur of the moment to have her hair done. So she was a little late when she arrived, looked flushed and pretty, at Cosimo's, close by the Moana Pool.

Sandy rose from the table. 'I began to wonder if you weren't taking it seriously again. There's a certain elusiveness about you, Erica Ryall!'

The Italian waiter settled her in her chair and handed her the menu. She buried herself behind it and said a breathless 'Yes ... yes ...' to everything Sandy or the waiter suggested.

'Still not the right weather to go for a sail,' he said, looking out of the big windows at the cloudy sky. 'It's going to be too late to help us if it does clear up.'

'Perhaps it's just as——' She broke off abruptly.

'What were you going to say?'

She dissolved into laughter. 'I was going to say, perhaps it's just as well. I quite forgot about the sailing trip and had my hair done!'

'Very nice it looks too,' he said, joining her laughter. 'It would be a pity to get it all blown about. But what *are* we going to do with the afternoon?'

'What do you usually do with a free afternoon?'

'Depends. If I'm working on a paper, I may have research to do at the University. Or there might be a lecture I want to attend. If the weather's good I go sailing. If it's bad I can always find some odd jobs in the flat, or I go to a concert——'

'Nothing on today,' Erica remarked.

'Do you like music?'

'Adore it! Concertos—especially piano concertos.'

'Do you play?'

'Yes, but I'm only good at playing pop. Isn't it maddening?'

'Pop is all right. I've got some jolly *good* pop records.'

'Rock, blues or what?'

'Oh, trendy, eh! Tamla Motown's my favourite——'

For a while they argued the pros and cons of derivative blues. When they remembered to look at the weather again, it was still murky.

'Soupy,' said Sandy. 'Dear, dear, it's always the same when I've got time off. "Oh Wild Wind, when will you blow——" '

'—"That the small rain down shall rain",' Erica finished. 'And that's just what's happening. It's turning to rain.'

'Look here, how about that film at the Regina? The epic about Ancient Rome?'

'I'd like that very much. Quite a lot of my favourite actors are in it.'

'You'll probably need a telescope to see them on the wide screen,' he teased. 'You know old Robb Tarryton— he was a patient in the men's medical when you were on that half of the ward——'

'Yes, that eczema case.'

'He went to see this film. He was telling me all about it in Outpatients the other day. Said he was glad the screen was so wide because in close-up it made the actresses look "mair o' a armfu' ".'

'I think you have to book up in advance, though, Sandy.'

'Oh, I expect there'll be seats. Not so many people go to the matinées.'

Erica asked after old Mr Tarryton, who had been a pet of hers in Furness Ward. This led them on to talk shop, so that Sandy had to call a taxi to get them to the Regina in time.

They enjoyed *Emperor of Rome* although they both agreed it was too long and the soundtrack too noisy.

'I don't know about you,' Sandy said as they came out into Princes Street, 'but what I need after all those gladiators and dancing girls is a nice strong cup of tea.'

'I second the motion!'

Daylight was fading, taking with it the last of the fog. The air was mild, damp, and fresh.

'I'll tell you what. Of course it's too late to go sailing, but there's enough light left to look at *Duenna*. She's in the boathouse under my flat. Then we could go upstairs and make some tea. How about that?'

She fell in with the idea at once. On the way there he explained some of the points of dinghy-sailing. 'I'm not such a dyed-in-the-wool enthusiast as some,' he admitted. 'I keep it up as a way of leaving the hospital and all its cares behind me.'

'Cares? I'd have said you let nothing get you down.'

'You're not the first person to say that to me, Erica. I sometimes get the impression that people think of me as a well-oiled watch!'

'But I can't honestly say I've ever thought of you as easily depressed.'

'If you had, would you have leapt to offer me your sympathy, as you did to Ian Dugall?'

She smiled and gave a little shrug, then said, 'I'm sorry if I spoke sharply to you the other day.'

'Don't apologise.' He took her arm to guide her among

44

the throng of home-going office and shop workers. 'It gave me something to think about.'

'About Ian, you mean? Sandy, if you'd get to know him a bit——'

'Not about Ian—about you. Until you put me in my place that day, I'd never been aware of you except as the pleasant and efficient nurse in Allerdyce.' They turned the corner into a little alley which led to the west side of the harbour. 'I'm rather glad it happened,' he said, and his words had a curious weight in the quietness of the lane. 'We wouldn't be here now, if it hadn't happened.'

She knew this was true. She wondered if he realised how big a step he'd taken.

'I've enjoyed today,' he went on. 'It's a long time since I've done anything like it.'

'I know,' she said, nodding.

'Meaning that I'm quite famous for the way I steer clear of afternoons at the cinema with pretty girls? Oh,' he added without rancour as she shook her head, 'the other blokes all chaff me about it. But it wasn't a well-laid plan to avoid gossip. I don't give a hoot about gossip. It's just that I've never found a girl who interested me—until now.'

They had reached the boathouse. He asked her to wait by the jetty while he sculled *Duenna* round into what remained of the daylight. She was a fourteen-foot X-class Jellicoe, her fresh blue paint glowing almost luminous in the dusk.

'I generally work her with a mainsail, forestaysail, and jib. Come aboard and get the feel of her,' he invited.

He held out his hand and, taking it, she jumped down into the little yacht. But the waves swelled, and she missed her footing as she landed. He caught her quickly, steadying her.

He could have let her go at once. Yet it was a long moment before he took his arm away. She looked up at him, and they studied each other gravely.

'Perhaps this isn't the moment for talking about sailing,' he said with a sudden smile. 'Come on, let's go indoors.'

He handed her ashore again. They went up the wooden staircase in silence. Inside, the spacious, airy room sprang to life as he went round it, switching on lamps and drawing curtains. He took her coat and laid it over a chairback.

'Let's get one thing straight before we go any further,' he said with a quiet decisiveness. 'This chap Ian Dugall—does he mean anything to you?'

It wasn't a question Erica could answer easily. 'He—he's a friend of mine,' she stammered.

'No more than that?'

'Well . . . It's difficult to explain. You see, he hasn't any other friends.'

'Whose fault is that?' Sandy asked with some impatience.

'His own—I know that. He has a very unfortunate manner——'

'But your feeling of friendship is strong enough to outweigh that.'

'I hope so. *Someone's* got to help him, Sandy.'

He moved restlessly. 'It seems to me he's got very little to worry about. He did well in his Finals. He's a capable enough physician. His father's name in itself is a recommendation in this part of the world. Honestly, Erica, he's better off than a lot of men——'

'Except that he lacks the knack of making friends.'

'But why does that mean *you* have to befriend him?'

46

'Does it matter so much?'

He waited a second before replying. 'I've a feeling it may come to matter a good deal.'

Erica sank down on a chair. She was tremendously confused; something in Sandy's way of speaking seemed to suggest that she could be of great importance to him. Despite herself, she felt a surge of elation. To think that Sandy could be so concerned about her friendship—it was like a dream come true!

Had he pressed her for a decision then—asked her point-blank not to go out with Ian again—she would have submitted. She had liked and admired Sandy from a distance so long that she'd have given up almost anything to have his close companionship.

But when he spoke again it was to say with some embarrassment, 'I've got a nerve, haven't I, prying into your affairs? Let's forget the whole thing. What about that tea we were going to make?'

She was glad to escape from the situation so easily. She followed him to the kitchen and put on the kettle while he got out cups and saucers. When he had done so he said, 'You know, I'm hungry. Are you?'

'I am, a bit.'

'What shall we do—drink the tea and go out to look for a place to eat? Or are you any good with a frying pan? I've probably got stuff in the fridge that we could cook.'

'What kind of stuff?'

'Let's go and have a look.' He opened the fridge door. Then he grinned suddenly. 'This might be the end of a glorious friendship. Mrs Catterell, my neighbour, has warned me that if ever I let another woman meddle in "her" kitchen she'll hand in her notice. And I couldn't get on without Mrs Catterell!'

'Do you manage your own breakfast? I see you're well stocked up on breakfast foods.'

'I'll let you into a secret—bacon and eggs is my favourite dish. I discovered it when I first came here as a boy and now I eat it at every meal when I'm on my own.'

'Then let's have that now. Shall we eat in the kitchen?'

'I usually do, to tell the truth. Saves a lot of work. Do you think that shows a sloppy attitude to life?'

'Oh, no—I love kitchens. Ours at home is the nicest room in the house.'

'I can't say the same for the one my mother reigns over. It's severely functional. My father insists she has all the latest labour-saving devices, which make it look like a power station or a factory. But she puts up with it because she knows it makes him happy. Where we come from, it was all old oaken tables and porcelain stoves for cooking.'

'Your father isn't a doctor, is he?'

'No, a fruit farmer. So are my two brothers. I'm the odd man out. Which is why,' he added, 'I sometimes seem to take the work rather seriously. I had to argue my father out of a conviction that I ought to be a farmer too. It's what we used to do back home in Hungary. Did your people have any objections when you decided to be a nurse?'

'We-ll, Mother was a bit doubtful. I'm the middle one of a family of five, so she knew I could stand up to the rough and tumble all right. But she thought I was too soft-hearted—she thought I'd never be able to be firm with the patients.'

'Generous-hearted would be a pleasanter term than soft-hearted,' he corrected, smiling. 'It's funny, Erica, but I'm not a bit surprised to hear you come from a big family.'

'Why? Do I look as if I've had to fight for my rights

since I was born?' she laughed.

'No, but there's a warmth about you . . . I should think yours is a very happy family.'

'Oh, it is.' She told him about her brother Richard's talent as an interior decorator, and how much he helped her father in the business. 'Dad keeps a furniture shop—Richard's persuaded him to go in for these lovely Scandinavian designs. My elder sister's just got married. Dad gave her the most *beautiful* stereo.'

'Mine's rather a nice design,' Sandy said. 'Come and have a look.'

She followed him into the living room. 'How about some music? I've got some good piano concertos,' he reminded her, laughing. 'Or how about dance music?'

He put on a record of Latin-American music. The irresistible rhythm filled the room, the plaintive trills of the flute embroidering it with a silvery magic. Sandy held out his hands; she took them, and he drew her against him as they began to dance.

Ideally, Erica should have been three or four inches taller to make a perfect dancing partner. But she was so light on her feet, so responsive to every least movement, that the difference in their heights ceased to matter.

While the record lasted they danced, speaking seldom, drawn closer by their ability to share the keen pleasure of perfect timing and rhythm. The physical contact made a difference to their relationship too. Erica was supremely conscious of an understanding, a dependence, growing up between them. The strength of his arm across her back, the gentle pressure with which he guided their steps—these brought intuitive knowledge of a man who could be both gentle and strong.

When the music throbbed to a close he held her for another moment. Her head was against his shoulder, and

49

after a while she looked up.

'That was perfect,' she said. 'Thank you.'

'It's I who should thank you,' he murmured. 'And for more than just dancing with me.'

He went to the stereo, picked up another record, then put it to one side.

'Let's not spoil it,' he said softly. 'We have all the time in the world ahead of us. Let's stop now, so that we can look forward all the more to our next dance.'

'When will that be, Sandy?'

'Tomorrow night? We could go to the Waikopua.'

'Oh, but everybody goes there. I mean, hospital staff——'

'And does that matter?'

'You know what they'll say, if they see us together?'

'I don't care what they say,' he replied with a faint shake of his brown head. 'Do you?'

'Not if you don't.'

'Then that's settled. Come on now—I'll take you home. The long way,' he added mischievously.

They wandered hand in hand through the quiet streets of Dunedin, speaking when they had anything to say, but quite happy to be silent. Erica's mind was busy with a million new, half-formed ideas which seemed likely to transfigure her outlook on life.

At the gate of the Nurses' Home they stopped. She knew he would kiss her goodnight, and trembled. It could be a kiss that demanded her love, and if she returned it she would be irrevocably committed. Sudden panic hit her. She had dreamed of Sandy falling in love with her, like a schoolgirl dreaming of a fairy prince. Did she want the reality?

As if he divined her feelings his goodnight kiss was gentle.

'We've got all the time in the world,' he repeated huskily. 'Goodnight, Erica my dear.'

Indoors there were several nurses listening to the radio in the sitting room. It was only a little before ten o'clock. But Erica escaped to her room and sat down, dazed yet happy, to think about the day just ending.

That Sandor Legrady should be falling in love with *her*——! How could it happen? Why should it happen? 'Why me?' she asked herself in wonder. And the only answer she could think of was that it was Sandy's own choice.

At length she began preparations for bed, but was interrupted by the arrival of Marion.

'So there you are! Where have you been all day?'

'Oh . . . shopping. Then I had lunch and—and went to the movies. What did you do this evening?' She avoided speaking of Sandy.

'Tom Quillan took me ten-pin bowling,' Marion said, blushing a little.

'Did he, indeed? Did you enjoy it?'

'Well, one thing's certain—it's good for getting rid of the spare inches!' She patted her Junoesque hips. Then she snapped her fingers in recollection. 'By the way, Ian Dugall rang you.'

'When was that?'

'Just after I came off duty. I took the call and told him you hadn't got back from your day out. He said to tell you he'd got tickets for next week.'

'Tickets for what? Did he say?'

'I don't remember—no, he didn't mention.' Marion sat down on Erica's bed and eyed her with curiosity. 'What goes on between you and King Dugall?' she demanded.

'Don't call him that, Marion!'

'Ooh, temper, temper! But why are you getting yourself

involved with him, my pet? Couldn't you choose someone a bit less stuck-up?'

'He isn't stuck-up——'

'He is too! He orders the nurses about like a general——'

'Only when they try to tease him——'

'Tease him? He never gives them the chance. This morning he had Goodrich nearly in tears. He's got a down on that child——'

'What else does she expect, when he caught her mimicking him?'

'Too bad! Is he the only doctor who's had that happen? If a man can't take a joke——'

'He's right to keep after Goodrich. She's inclined to slack, as you'll find out when you've had her on your ward a while longer.'

'So you've got a down on the poor kid too? Have you forgotten what it was like to be a first-year pro.?'

'No, I haven't. And I remember very well that I jumped to attention when a doctor, a sister or a senior nurse spoke——'

'Well, Goodrich does that. It's only a great I-am like Dr Dugall who——'

'If you're going to take her side against him——!'

'Certainly I'm going to take her side! It's not just Goodrich he bosses, in any case. Nobody likes him, not even the other doctors.'

'It's just because they haven't got to know him. If they——'

'Don't be silly! They got his measure inside the first week. I'm sure Tom's the kindest-hearted chap you'd ever meet, but even he can't stand Ian Dugall. If he's not letting them know how wonderful he is, he's telling them how wonderful his father was.'

'I used to feel the same way, but once you get to know him——'

'Why bother? Why burden yourself with a friendship like that? It's all very well to fancy yourself as noble and sympathetic and the rest of us as prejudiced, but has it ever occurred to you that we may be right and you may be wrong? If you'll take my advice——'

'You're not offering advice, you're passing judgments,' Erica said hotly, 'and on things you know nothing about! You've never exchanged a word with Ian except inside the ward. I've been out with him——'

'Once only as I recall. How you can know so much about him after only one evening, I can't fathom!'

'At least I know a bit more than you do—and I don't set myself to give a character reading on him, as some people do.'

'In other words, mind my own business?' said Marion, getting even more pink.

'If you like to put it like that—yes.'

'All right.' Marion marched to the door. 'I hope you find Ian Dugall a consolation when you've lost all your friends!'

She went out, closing the door ungently. Erica started after her, but changed her mind with her hand on the door knob. She couldn't apologise to Marion, she was still too indignant. Tomorrow, when they had both cooled off a little. . . .

Next day outside the ward doors she caught Ian's eye as he hurried past. He broke step.

'I got your message about the tickets,' she said. 'Sorry I was still out when you rang.'

'Your sailing lesson didn't come off, I suppose? You said it wouldn't.'

'No-o, I didn't go sailing.'

'What did you do? It was a beastly day.'

'As a matter of fact——' She wavered. But why should she be averse from telling him how she'd spent her day? 'As a matter of fact, Sandy took me to see that epic at the Regina.'

She saw his face change. 'At the Regina?'

'Yes. What's the matter?'

'Nothing—only—— Oh, nothing.'

A horrible idea struck her. 'Ian, it wasn't tickets for the Regina——? Oh, Ian!' She could see that was exactly what had happened. 'Oh, I am sorry. It just didn't occur to me. When you said tickets for a show, I thought you meant a theatre.'

'There's nothing good on at the theatre next week— just a touring company with one of those depressing plays. Never mind——'

'We can still go to the Regina. I don't mind seeing *Emperor of Rome* again. In fact, I'd like to——'

'Don't be absurd. I wouldn't inflict that on you.'

'But the tickets—it's a pity to waste them——'

'One of the chaps may be willing to take them off me. I heard Tom Quillan say he wouldn't mind seeing the film. The thing is, we're a bit limited for choice now. You know the town better than I do—what do you recommend?'

'Let me think——'

'Listen, I've got to rush off—I'm expected in Furness. But I could get out for a coffee this evening. Shall we discuss it then?'

'Oh. Well, this evening, as a matter of fact——'

'You've got a date?'

'Well—yes.'

'Not with Sandy Legrady, by any chance?' he said in sardonic inquiry. 'Look, Erica, I'm sorry. I'm wanted elsewhere. Let's skip the whole thing, shall we?'

The busy life of a big hospital throws people together; but it also gives them an excuse to avoid speaking except on hospital matters. For the rest of that day, although Erica tried for a chance, she and Ian never exchanged a word on any subject but the patients.

'What did I tell you?' Marion said triumphantly, having watched Ian walk past with a cool nod as the girls went in to late lunch. 'You can't depend on him at all.'

'Oh, you don't understand, Marion. Those tickets he spoke of are for that film at the Regina, and as ill luck would have it I went to see it yesterday afternoon.'

'Still, need he be so cool to you?'

'But you see, when he suggested we should meet tonight to discuss what else we could do next week, I'd already got a date.'

'For this evening? Where are you going?'

'To the Waikopua.'

'Dancing? Who with?' Marion raised her eyebrows.

'With—with Sandy Legrady.'

'With Sandy?' Marion exclaimed, so loudly that the other occupants of the dining room looked round. 'You're joking!'

'No, Marion, I'm not.'

'With Sandy? Who else is going?'

'Nobody.'

'Nobody? Just the two of you? We-ell! You sly old thing! How long has this been going on?' her friend demanded with delight.

'Oh, for goodness' sake, Marion, don't make so much of it——'

'Don't be a goose. You know as well as I do that Sandy wouldn't take a girl out unless . . . Come on, tell me all. Is tonight the first time?'

'The first time we've gone out dancing. But I went out with him yesterday afternoon.'

'Then it was Sandy who took you to see the Roman thing?'

'Yes, and now poor Ian is landed with tickets for next week——'

'I'll tell Tom. He's quite keen to see it. How was it—any good? Or were you too overwhelmed to notice?'

'Oh, Marion, please don't——!'

'Don't mind me, duckie. I'm just so surprised that I can't take it in. You've kept it such a dead secret——'

'But there's nothing in it, really, Marion. I mean, just because we go out together——'

'Am I the first to hear?' Marion asked, looking triumphant.

'Except for Ian.'

'Mmm . . . No wonder Ian is looking so huffy; he's got some fierce competition, hasn't he? Lord, wait till this gets round!'

It was what Erica dreaded. This feeling of being on public view nearly made her turn and run when she entered the Waikopua Restaurant on Sandy's arm. But somehow, once they began to dance, her worries faded. The former magic returned. She was happy.

So Marion told her when she got home that night. 'You're so happy you've got stars in your eyes, my dear.'

'Have I?' Erica put her hands to her flushed cheeks and went to look at herself in the mirror. Stars—yes, they were there.

'You must admit it was more enjoyable than being with your other boy-friend,' Marion hinted.

'But that's quite different——' She broke off. 'Oh, poor Ian,' she murmured regretfully. 'It seems unjust that I should be so happy and he should be so miserable. I absolutely must make an opportunity to talk to him in the morning.'

'While you're about it, you might get him to apologise to Tom.'

'Apologise? What for?' Erica felt her heart begin to sink. The evening's enchantment was already banished.

'If he's going to speak like that to Tom when Tom was only trying to do him a favour——!'

'Speak like what? What's Tom been doing?'

'Well, you know how you said we ought to try to make friends with Ian and everything. Tom thought he'd show willing, by offering to buy those tickets for the cinema. Now what harm was there in that?'

'It would have been better if you'd let me handle it—— Well, go on.'

'Ian asked how Tom knew he had any tickets. Tom said he understood Ian had bought them, but wasn't going to use them because you'd already seen the film. Ian said he didn't like having his affairs discussed by all and sundry. He told Tom to mind his own confounded business.'

'Where was this?'

'In the doctors' sitting-room. It made Tom look an awful fool, Erica, because it appears he'd been passing on what I told him about trying to get to know Ian just before Ian came in. Tom's very vexed with me, Erica.'

'I'm terribly sorry, Marion.'

'So you ought to be, you and that horrible man you insist on defending. It's all your fault, Erica!'

CHAPTER FOUR

THE hospital's dining hall was a communal affair: medical staff one end, nursing staff the other. Erica lingered over breakfast until she saw Ian come in the door from the residents' quarters. Then she hurried off to her ward to take report from the night staff, started her juniors on the day's work, and sped back to the main corridor in time to waylay Ian as he came out.

'I want to talk to you,' she said without preamble.

'I'm afraid I——'

'It won't take a minute—it mustn't, because I've got to get back to Allerdyce. This way.'

She acted with such determination that he automatically followed her through the door to the Inner Quadrangle. There was a lawn here, bordered by geraniums whose brilliant scarlet issued a gay defiance against the coolness of New Zealand's March weather.

'Well?' said Ian.

'I hear you were beastly rude to Tom Quillan last night.'

'Ah, the tom-toms have been beating, have they?'

'If you have a public quarrel you must expect to have it talked about.'

'Public or private, it makes no difference. Everybody knows your business and chats about it. I suppose half the hospital know by now that I bought tickets to take you to a film you'd already seen with Legrady.'

'Would it be so bad if they did know?' she asked bluntly.

'Not for you. I've no doubt you're glorying in the triumph of captivating Reidmouth's most eligible bachelor.'

He saw her mouth tremble and knew he had hurt her. When she reached for his hand, he let her take it.

'You're trying to quarrel with me,' she reproached him softly. 'I thought we were going to be friends?'

'So did I, but how can we if you're going to be so taken up with Legrady?'

'It depends what you mean by "so taken up". If you ask me to go out for a cup of coffee with you tonight so we can discuss what to do next week, I'll say yes.'

'You mean it? You really want to? I mean about next week too? I thought you wouldn't have time, now that——What I mean is, people are saying he's not the type to play around, so if he's taking you out it's—well, it's serious. So you won't be wanting to bother with me.'

'Ian dear, I suppose you don't mean to be insulting,' she teased, 'but I'm not keen on this idea that I offer friendship one day and cancel the offer the next because it's too much bother.'

'Oh, Erica . . .' He gave a half-laugh. 'It does sound awful, put like that!'

'Meet you tonight in the Barbecue, then?'

'About seven. Right, that's fine. I'm—I'm awfully glad.' He screwed himself up for the next sentence. 'Erica, I'm sorry for the way I behaved to you.'

'I'd rather you said that to Tom Quillan. Will you, Ian?'

'Apologise, you mean?' Clearly he didn't like the idea.

'You *were* rude to him, Ian. And he was only trying to be friendly.'

'He had no business to stick his nose into my affairs!'

'If that's how you feel, it's no use urging you.' She

pressed his hand and turned to go indoors. 'I must fly—
it's a hard life trying to run a ward when you're not a
hard-hearted Sister! See you tonight.'

'Erica——'

'Yes?'

'All right, I'll tell Quillan I'm sorry.'

She was smiling to herself as she hurried upstairs. To
have persuaded this tense, proud young man to apologise
was a great step forward. For his sake, not for her own,
she was pleased.

When she reached Allerdyce she found Sandy waiting
for her. It was too early for rounds, and he'd armed himself with some reports from the Path. Lab. as an excuse to
come calling.

'I must be in a daze,' he greeted her. 'I never made
any arrangements before we parted last night. What
would you like to do this evening?'

'Aren't you on duty this evening?' she parried, in some
dismay.

'On call. Where would you like to go?'

'I'm not free this evening, Sandy. I'm sorry.' She
decided to get the whole explanation out in one fell swoop.
'I've made arrangements to meet Ian for a cup of
coffee.'

'Made arrangements? When?'

'Just this minute.'

'Erica, this is ridiculous! Surely you knew I'd be asking
you?'

'I didn't think about it. I was worried about something
else. There was a bit of a fracas in the doctors' sitting-
room last night.'

'So I've just heard. But I'm hanged if I see——'

'I've got to talk to him. There's a lot I've got to explain.'

60

'Oh, I see.' He looked happier. 'You mean this is the last time?'

Erica's blue eyes showed her surprise. 'Why should it be?'

'Well, I thought—— At least I'd hoped—— You won't be going out with him again, surely?'

'But I shall. I promised to be a friend to him.'

'Yes, but that was *before*—— Things are different now, Erica—aren't they?'

Before she could reply the telephone in Sister's office began to ring. As Acting Sister it was Erica's job to answer it. She made as if to go.

'Wait, now,' Sandy commanded. 'This is important.'

'I've got to answer that, Sandy——'

'You won't be coming out with me tonight?'

'No, I'm afraid not. I'm sorry if you'd counted on it.'

Nurse Mackie, the third-year nurse, put her head round the door. 'Matron on the phone, Staff.'

'Yes, I'm coming.' She stepped towards the office.

Sandy went with her. 'Look here,' he said, with some irony, 'it seems I have to put my word in early, so what are you planning to do with your free time tomorrow and Sunday?'

'Saturday I'm on until tea-time. Sunday I'm free.'

'Can we go dancing on Saturday evening?'

'I'd love that, Sandy.'

'And we might try sailing on Sunday afternoon if the weather's passable.'

'Yes—that would be nice——' Her mind was divided between what Sandy was saying and the august personage waiting for her on the telephone.

'That'll give you Sunday evening free for your good neighbour policy with Ian,' Sandy said as a parting shot, with a fair attempt at a laugh.

At tea Marion reported that Tom had had an apology from Ian. 'Not a very friendly one,' she grumbled. 'He did it rather formally, in front of everybody in the doctors' sitting-room.'

'That was only fair, I suppose, since the argument was a public thing,' Erica defended.

'Tom said it was frightfully embarrassing. Really, Erica, your pet lamb is an awful problem child!'

Erica was growing more and more aware of the 'awful problems' in which she'd involved herself. That evening she made a careful explanation to Ian of the situation as she saw it: he was completely understanding and reasonable about the whole thing, but then threw her off balance by saying, 'What about Sandy, though?'

'What about him?'

'I'm only too glad to have your friendship. But is Sandy going to see it that way? I've noticed his eye on me more than once today—as if he were trying to work out exactly how serious a rival I am.'

'Sandy understands everything completely. I told him this morning that I should go on seeing you.'

She should have taken warning from her own smug self-satisfaction. The situation was much too delicate to be so neatly solved. As Sunday was to prove to her.

The plan to go sailing with Sandy had to be abandoned once more. 'The weather always seems at its worst at weekends,' he sighed, 'especially at this time of year. What would you like to do instead?'

'There's a concert at the Town Hall—Russian music. Does that sound all right?'

'I had a look at the programme in the paper, actually. It's Rimsky-Korsakov, Tchaikovsky, and Rachmaninov—the second piano concerto,' he added with a grin of recollection. 'And afterwards we'll have a meal at Cosimo's.'

'Oh—well—Sandy, I can't do that——'

'Why not?'

'I—well, I have to get back to the hospital——'

A shadow crossed his features. 'To meet Ian?'

She nodded, vexed at the way this news seemed to damp their enjoyment.

But she was revived by the glorious warmth of sound that filled the concert-hall. All the romantic emotions of the Russian soul seemed to surge through the strings, sighing and rejoicing, appealing and triumphing. Erica sat with her hand lightly clasped in Sandy's, her eyes half closed. Now and again, when she struggled free of the music's spell, she would glance at Sandy to see if he shared her enjoyment. Each time she did so, she found his eyes on her face.

They walked from the Town Hall steps without consciously choosing a direction. The wind and rain were still carousing round the town, lashing the rata and the trees to and fro, but in the Town Belt they found shelter under a rustic summer-house, where a few rambler roses were still in blossom.

' " 'Tis the last rose of summer",' quoted Erica, gently touching one with her forefinger and watching a rain spattered petal flutter to the ground. 'Strange to have summer ending in March instead of September.'

Sandy captured her hand and put it against his cheek. To her amazement, she realised he was trembling.

'I love you, Erica,' he said in a low voice. 'I never thought I'd ever say that to any woman and mean it so deeply. I can't get you out of my mind. You're with me night and day—you've been with me ever since that first time we spent the afternoon together. I'm lost, Erica—lost in a sea of love and longing. What am I to do?'

Her fingers stroked his cheek. She was greatly troubled

by the pain she could see in his eyes. This was not how she had imagined love; he looked haggard.

'What's wrong, my dear? Why do you look like that?'

He turned his head so that he could kiss her fingers. 'Oh, my darling—if you could only care for me——'

'But, Sandy, I *do*——'

He took her in his arms and brought his mouth down on hers. He kissed her with a passion that seemed to tear at the very roots of his being. When he let her go, he was shaking.

'But not like that,' he said. 'You like me—you're fond of me—don't pretend, Erica! I know it's not the same for you as it is for me. Heaven knows I never wanted this to happen. Sometimes I wish I'd never stopped to speak to you that day I noticed you and Ian . . . When I think it was mere curiosity that prompted me to question you— mere idle curiosity.' When in the grip of emotion, as he was now, a slight hint of his Hungarian accent came back. He laughed a little. 'Now I know how it's possible for curiosity to kill the cat—I've caught myself in a death-trap with mine!'

She was frightened, bewildered. 'But what is it? What's wrong? Darling, I don't want you to be unhappy! Tell me what's wrong.'

She had a glimpse of his tortured face before he hid it against her hair.

'I'm jealous,' he whispered. 'I can't help myself—it must have something to do with the Hungarian blood in my veins. I can't bear to think of you so much as smiling at another man. Erica, if you care for me at all—promise me——'

'What?' she said in dismay, for she already guessed what he was going to ask.

'Promise me to stop seeing Ian Dugall!'

Erica held Sandy fast in her arms, her heart overflowing with love and pity. To have to make such an appeal——— She knew he must despise himself, she knew that only desperation had wrung it from him. He wasn't the kind of man to give in to this degrading emotion of jealousy without having struggled until his strength was exhausted.

Yet his love was so great that his jealousy couldn't be conquered. Despite herself, she was conscious of a thrill of wonder. He loved her so greatly—he turned to her, of all women, he who could have made his choice among a score of willing hearts.

She stroked his brown hair gently. 'There's no need to be jealous of Ian. Truly, Sandy, you're torturing yourself needlessly.'

He shook his head without looking up, so that his lips moved against her temple.

'You may believe that, but I know better.'

'But there's nothing to know! I like Ian, and I want to help him—and that's all there is to it.'

'And you think that's so little?' He straightened and moved away a fraction, so that he could look down into her eyes. 'That's a great deal, my sweet darling. You don't know how strong that hold could grow on a generous heart like yours. Please—I implore you—give him up now, before it harms us both!'

'But how can you ask that? How can you be so afraid of a man who means you no harm? There's no reason why Ian and I shouldn't go on just being friends for the rest of our lives.'

'No, every friendship changes—it either grows or it dies. For some unfathomable reason you feel that Ian needs you—I don't know why you think so, but I know you believe it because I've seen the way your eyes soften when you speak of him, and the way you fly to his defence if he's attacked.' He gave her a singularly grave, sweet smile. 'Little tough guy,' he murmured with a break in his voice.

She returned the smile, feeling a relaxation in the tension between them. If Sandy loved her, surely he must trust her.

'I do believe Ian needs me. I can't tell you the reason—he wouldn't want me to tell anyone else. But he does need a friend and he'll continue to do so, perhaps for the rest of his stay in Reidmouth. You wouldn't want me to turn my back on him after I promised?'

'Yes,' Sandy said urgently, 'yes, that's what I want you to do! Don't you see—it's that promise you made that terrifies me. Think what a hold it gives him. He's alone, you think he's unhappy, no one likes him, you're the only one he can turn to—don't you see? The more you give him your sympathy, the more he'll need you. And the greater his demands upon you, the farther you drift from me.'

'But that's not strictly logical, Sandy——'

'Logical?' he burst out despairingly. 'Oh, you don't love me or you wouldn't talk about logic. What has logic to do with it? I tell you I *know*—I know that if you go on seeing Ian you'll get fonder of him——'

'Even if that were true, it needn't be a thing for you to fear.'

He moved away from her, and gave a shrug that was typically European. 'Why can't I make you see?' He waited a moment, then went on, 'It's because you don't love me——'

'But——'

'Oh no, Erica, don't shake your head. You don't love me as I love you. You feel a great warmth and affection for me, but when I kissed you a moment ago it meant relatively little. Your head reeled a little and you felt a

66

tingle in the blood—that's good, I'm glad—but heavens above, you don't confuse that with being in love? Give me your hand.'

She obeyed, and he put it against his heart. She could feel the unsteady pounding there.

'That's love, Erica. I don't want your affection, your respect and admiration, your friendship even. I want to hear your heart beat like that when I take you in my arms. And it could be like that—I could make you love me in time. But a voice inside me keeps whispering "You'll lose her. He'll win in the end."'

'How? What do you mean?' She had never felt so bewildered; it was like being lost in a vast unknown country.

'I think that at the moment Ian and I stand about equal in your affections. The ironic thing is, I think he holds all the advantages. He needs you, so you believe. Not only that but, because there's no one else he could turn to, you're *indispensable*. And your protective emotions are all aroused for him—you have to fight his battles for him. Whereas I——' his voice filled with weariness—'I have everything, haven't I? I have a host of friends and I've had to learn to stand on my own two feet. If it came to a choice, you'd stand by the one who would have nothing without you. And it will come to a choice, Erica, I know it will. Ian's already falling in love with you and he won't want to share you for long.'

'You're wrong, Sandy——'

'I know I'm right.'

'But Ian isn't like that. He doesn't want to monopolise me——'

'Not yet. He knows he only has to wait, though, till his claim is strong enough. I've watched him. He calculates every move he makes.'

'How can you be so unjust?' she cried. 'You've only seen one side of him. He isn't what you think—he's worried and unsure of himself, and as for claiming me— why, he told me himself that he understood you came first.'

'And do I?'

'Why—why, you know that if——'

'If it were put to the test, I would win? If I insisted you must stop seeing Ian, you'd agree?'

'I hope you won't do that, Sandor,' she said gravely.

'No, because you know you'd have to refuse, and you don't want to quarrel with me.' He smiled bitterly. 'I knew this was how it would go. Before I spoke about Ian, I knew you would never give him up. Yet somehow I couldn't prevent myself from pleading with you. . . .' He took a grip on himself and made a valiant attempt at banter. 'It's all that Russian music—it takes the emotional brakes off a temperamental Magyar like me and leaves me careering along out of control.'

'Sandor, I give you my word that you have nothing to worry about.'

'You really are a sweetheart,' he replied gently. 'I think you honestly believe that. Well, come on—I've finished making a fool of myself for today. Let's go and get some tea, so that you'll be in time for your evening date.'

He seemed to want a chance to retreat a little, into mocking acceptance of a situation he couldn't alter. Erica fell in with his wishes.

Soon after six they left the café where they had had tea. 'What time are you—what time is your appointment?' Sandy inquired.

'About seven.'

'Shall I get seats for the concert next Sunday?'

'If you would like to.' She was beginning to feel tongue-

68

tied with embarrassment.

'Forgive me?' he asked.

'For what?'

'For behaving like a typical Middle-European lover. It shan't happen again, I promise.'

Erica suddenly clung heavily to his arm and gazed up at him, her eyes filling. 'Oh, Sandy, dearest—I'm so sorry. It's all my fault, isn't it?'

'Not a bit. It's my fault. And now I've made you cry. What's Ian going to say when he sees you with your eyes all red? He'll come and knock my block off.'

'No, he won't. I'll tell him that it's all because of that sentimental Russian music.' She blinked hard, and vanquished the tears. 'There—that better?'

'Couldn't be better when you were perfect to begin with.'

'Oh, Sandy!' She was blushing now.

'Don't you believe me? That's one of the things that's so wonderful about you, my dear. You're completely without conceit. Well, here we are.' He paused. 'I may kiss you goodnight?' he asked uncertainly.

'Oh, darling, of *course*!'

His lips lingered on hers for a long while. She tried to put love and reassurance into her response. When he turned to leave he was smiling.

If he had always been as calm as at that parting, Erica's life for the next few weeks would have been happier. She knew that he tried, desperately, to control his feelings. He tried not to show resentment when she had to refuse an invitation because of previous arrangements with Ian; he never asked where they had gone or what they'd done. His manner to Ian himself was much as it had always been—not friendly, because they had never been friends, yet not unfriendly either. He behaved as he thought a 'cold-blooded Anglo-Saxon' would behave.

But now and again there would be a flash that warned of the storm yet to come. And sometimes when he kissed Erica there was an almost angry demand behind his tenderness, as if he would *make* her love him.

Erica tried to ensure that when she was with one of them she never encountered the other. But in a town such as Dunedin, where the main life of the community revolves round the Octagon, this was almost impossible. From time to time it would happen that all three were in the same place at the same time.

One cold evening in late April Erica asked Ian to take her ten-pin bowling. Marion and Tom had taken this up in quite a big way, and Marion's enthusiasm had wakened Erica's interest. But when she and Ian had been struggling, amid laughter, to master the art of sending down a good curve for about half an hour, a large party from Reidmouth Hospital staff walked in. Marion and Tom were in the lead, but Sandy was one of the group.

Marion, who from time to time had fits of conscience about trying to get to know Ian, suggested the two parties should join. This would give two five-man teams, which seemed to be desirable, according to the custom.

But it was a mistake to mix. Ian had been quite happy to make a fool of himself and laugh at his mistakes with only Erica to watch him. But in front of the others—and especially in front of Sandy—it was different. Then, flustered by the ten-pin scoring methods, he queried Tom Quillan's score-keeping.

Tom was a brawny young man of Irish extraction, with red hair and a temper to match. He flared up. Sandy tried to smooth them both down.

'What does it matter about the score?' he said. 'We're all beginners.'

'But he as good as said I diddled him out of that "spare". Oh, I don't know,' Tom said in disgust, 'I'm always getting involved in public harangues with this bloke.'

'I'm quite willing to forgo the pleasure,' Ian said coldly.

'Come on, man, don't be difficult about it,' urged Sandy, and it was perhaps inevitable that he should address this remark to Ian rather than to Tom, though both were to blame.

Erica didn't improve matters by leaping to Ian's defence. 'Ian only asked Tom if he had marked in his "spare".'

'I heard him,' Sandy replied, with a swift glance at him. 'Tom had, of course—I don't know why he should question it.'

Ian shrugged. 'It's clear the mathematics of this game are beyond me,' he said, pretending nonchalance and doing it so well he sounded lordly. 'And really it hardly seems worth the effort. I think I'll sit out the rest and watch you.'

'But then one team will be a man short,' protested Tom in extreme annoyance.

'Then I'll drop out too,' said Erica. 'That'll even things up.'

'But you're getting so good at it, Erica,' Marion cried.

'Come on, Erica, stay with it,' Sandy urged. 'Don't spoil your evening——'

'I'm not really enjoying it any more,' she replied, colouring.

Sandy moved aside with her as she went towards the spectators' chairs. 'Oh, for heaven's sake, Erica, stop running round after him like a nursemaid. If he wants to sit out, let him.'

'He doesn't want to,' she said with resentment. 'We were having a grand time until the rest of you turned up and began muddling us up with rules and scores and all that.'

'In other words, we spoiled it.'

'Well, it certainly isn't any fun now.'

'I see,' he said grimly.

After that evening, the situation between the two men deteriorated. During their on-duty hours Ian was less co-operative than he should have been, tending to by-pass Sandy and ask instructions from his consultant. Sandy, on his side, was so painstakingly polite as to be almost insulting. The atmosphere between them was noticeable to everyone, even to Dr Galland. The consultant wasn't noted for his skill at personal contacts with his staff; so long as they did their work he preferred not to be bothered, and relied on his Registrar to settle any difficulties. When, however, he found difficulties being *caused* by his Registrar, he had to take action. And the easiest action was to reprimand his immediate junior. Being the tactless man he was, Dr Galland saw nothing wrong with saying loudly to Sandy in front of everyone, 'What's the matter with you these days, Legrady?'

'Nothing that I'm aware of, sir.'

'Then why does your houseman have to keep running to me with every little thing?'

'I'll see that it doesn't happen again,' Sandy said.

Erica, who knew the true state of affairs, couldn't help reproaching Ian that evening. 'You know you ought to ask Sandy for advice before you take it any further, Ian.'

'But he's so hostile, Erica.'

'He's not hostile. At least, not over the work. Sandy would never let anything affect his attitude to the work.

Now admit it, Ian—he's never been unreasonable or ex-acting——'

'No, but I have this awful feeling that he's watching me like a hawk. And I know why, too. It's not really to do with the work.'

Erica shivered and drew the collar of her topcoat close to her throat. It was a night more suitable for a fireside than a walk by the upper Harbour.

'You realise he's head over ears in love with you, Erica, don't you? Anyone can tell by watching him when you're around.'

'I don't want to discuss it——'

'But I think the time has come when we must. This enmity between Legrady and me is because of you. He resents sharing you with me.'

'It'll all work out in time——'

'Not before you're worn to a shadow by the worry of it. Erica, you care a good deal for him, don't you? And if I hadn't come on the scene you'd probably have been engaged to him by now.'

'If you hadn't come on the scene, ironically enough, Sandy would never have noticed me.'

'What on earth do you mean?'

'It doesn't matter. Anyhow, you *are* on the scene now——'

'But I can easily clear off it. We could stop seeing each other. It's as easy as that.'

It opened up before her—an easy road, an escape from this tangle of tensions and jealousies. 'But wouldn't you mind——?' she faltered.

'I'm a grown man, after all, my dear. I oughtn't to be having my hand held. And it's making you unhappy. I'd rather anything, almost, than see your eyes full of trouble. Just say the word, and I'll make myself scarce.'

She wavered. After all, there was truth in what he said about being a grown man. When he left Reidmouth, he would have to manage without her. Why not sooner? And she might be able to find peace—she wouldn't have to spend her life on this precarious tightrope any more.

But could she purchase peace at Ian's expense? She asked, 'Wouldn't you miss having someone to talk to?'

And at the lonely picture her own words conjured up, she was gripped by a sudden ache in her throat. She gave a sob. Next moment she was in tears—not only for Ian, but for herself and for Sandy, and the hopelessness of it all.

'Erica!' Ian cried. 'Erica, my dear, don't!' He put his arm around her and drew her against the shelter of his shoulder. 'Don't cry, darling. Please don't. I'll do anything, anything at all, to make you happy. I love you so much, it breaks my heart to see you cry. I've spoilt everything for you, haven't I, my darling, my precious? Don't, don't cry!'

Something of what he was saying penetrated her storm of emotion. She fought for control and looked up at him. The light from the old-fashioned street lamp shone on his face with a cool clarity.

She recognised what she saw there. But she asked the question. 'Did you say—you love me?'

'But I thought you knew that,' he said.

CHAPTER FIVE

By the time they had walked to the Vista Café, Erica was almost herself again. If the waitress was curious about the redness of her eyes, she concealed the fact and gave them her usual cheerful greeting. They were quite regular customers by now.

When she had brought their coffee they sat silent for a while.

'You'll think I'm a fool,' Erica said at length. 'But I never guessed that you—that you——'

'Perhaps it's not so surprising,' Ian admitted. 'I'm not a demonstrative sort of person. It probably didn't show as much as I thought it did.' He paused. 'But Legrady knows.'

'But how can he?'

'I don't know. He's got a sort of sixth sense about people, you see. It's what makes him such a good doctor.'

'What am I going to do?' she murmured. 'What on earth am I going to do?'

'Knowing that I'm in love with you makes a difference? Don't let it, Erica. It's your feelings that matter—only yours. Please, please believe me. All I want is for you to be happy.' He was deeply in earnest. His dark eyes were fixed on hers.

'But how can I be? Whatever I do, somebody's going to be hurt—and I hate hurting people——'

She bent her head. She busied herself with her coffee. Then she looked up and went on, 'You say you want me to be happy. What advice would you give me?'

He flushed. 'That's not fair, Erica.'

'I'm too tired to be fair. My mind's a jumble. I want to please everybody and not hurt anybody and yet do what's right. That's an impossibility. So what do you think I ought to do?'

'You really want my opinion?'

'Of course!'

'Even though it'll sound like backing out of what I said a moment ago?'

'You mean about not seeing each other?'

'That still stands if it's what you want, darling. If in the end you decide I'd be better out of your path, I'll step aside. But I think that would be a bad decision.'

'For whom?'

'For you. You'd be doing it to buy peace with Sandy. I wouldn't blame you, mind you—but peace at any price could be a mistake. Sandy is the type who's used to being in control. Once let him take over your life and choose your friends for you, and your independence is gone for ever. Don't forget, for all his cool manner, he's got stormy Hungarian ancestors.'

'But he's not like that,' she objected.

'I'm not saying he'd be domineering or unkind. But I think he'd edge out any friends who seemed to claim too much of your affection, probably without being aware of what he was doing. You can't deny that he's intensely jealous, Erica—you wouldn't be so miserable if he hadn't been making you unhappy out of sheer jealousy.'

'He hates himself for it,' she murmured, remembering Sandy's tortured face.

'I believe that. But he can't cope with it. If once he forces you to give in, he'll want to own you through and through. I've studied him, Erica. He's a man who's had control of his life up to now, but finds he's swept away by a force

76

stronger than his own self-discipline. For all the calmness of the exterior, there's a volcano underneath. That's why I haven't just quietly faded out of your life, although I guessed that, on the face of it, it would make things easier if I did. I felt that you had the right to choose your friends and direct your own life. I still say that if it's what you want, I'll step aside. But think before you say yes. You'd have to love Sandy with all your heart and soul before you could give yourself up to him as entirely as he'd want.'

'I can't understand how you know all this,' she said in wonder.

'Perhaps I'm developing some of Sandy's sixth sense. Perhaps it comes to your aid if you need it badly enough.'

She sighed and nodded. 'I wish I had it. Heaven knows I need it. It might have told me, perhaps, how you felt about me.'

'Don't let that worry you. I shan't make a nuisance of myself. I don't expect you to love me. Why should you?'

'I could give reasons,' she replied, covering his hand with her own. 'You're very honest, and very kind to me.'

'But that's not enough to fall in love with.' He patted her hand. 'If Sandy weren't around, I think my chances would be brighter. But I'm lucky for all that. At least you borrow my shoulder to cry on!'

'It won't happen again,' she assured him. 'And now let's forget all our worries and hear the good news you said you'd had.'

'Oh yes—in a letter from my mother. What d'you think? She's coming to Reidmouth for a week between filming TV commercials. "Resting", it's called.'

'I bet you're looking forward to it. When is she coming?'

'Saturday. I'm fixing up for her to stay at the Mawai

Hotel. She's dying to meet you, you know. That's nine-tenths of her reason for coming—she wants to see what sort of a person you are.'

Erica felt a little stab of apprehension. 'You haven't given her the impression that you and I——?'

'Oh no!—quite the reverse. I explained early on that you were as good as engaged to somebody else.'

'But that wasn't strictly true.'

'I thought it was at the time. I still do. But the point is, Mother wants to meet you and thank you for being so good to me.'

'Does she know how we came to get friendly? Have you told her your doubts about being in the wrong job?'

'Good God, no! And she mustn't know, Erica! You'll be careful not to mention it, won't you?'

Mrs Dugall arrived on Saturday and was met at the airport by her son, who had wangled a weekend off. Erica joined them for tea later in the day, a good deal more nervous than she would have admitted at the prospect of meeting the cool scrutiny of the woman in Ian's photograph.

But she needn't have feared. Nancy Dugall's brown eyes could be warm and friendly, especially to someone who had been kind to her son. At first, perhaps, there was wariness in her glance. But that vanished within the first five minutes.

'I've longed to meet you, Erica. Ian's letters have been full of you—but you know what men are like, they never answer questions! He never even described you when I asked what you looked like.'

'Oh, Mother, you know I'm not good at that sort of thing.'

'Your father was just the same. Brilliant doctors seem to be bad letter-writers.' She poured the tea, her fine hands strong and efficient. 'Ian always wanted to be a doctor, you know, Erica. Even when he was a little boy, he used to bandage up our dachshund. And if I missed him, I could generally run him to earth looking at the pictures in his father's medical books. Most unsuitable, some of them were!'

'Now you know the reason for all my complexes,' Ian said with a burst of laughter. 'I saw something nasty in a medical book when I was eleven!'

'You can laugh,' Nancy said with some seriousness, 'but you know you did cut yourself off from youngsters of your own age. When other children were out climbing trees or playing football, you were buried in a book. It made you awfully shy with people. Do you remember that red-headed girl student you took a shine to?'

'Vanessa, her name was,' he recalled. 'She married a dentist.'

'Tell me more,' begged Erica. 'Tell me all about his gaudy past.'

'No, it's only that he was really quite keen on this girl, but it took him so long to make up his mind to speak to her that somebody else got in first. Not that it matters, because I think she was matrimony-minded and I don't approve of early marriage.'

'You're a fine one to talk,' said her son. 'You were eighteen when Father rushed you up the aisle.'

'That's what I mean. I often wonder . . . Perhaps he mightn't have stayed in New Zealand if he'd been free. Perhaps he'd have gone on with his work in Polynesia.'

'I'm sure he never regretted it,' Erica said gently.

'Are you thinking of getting married soon?'

'Who to?' Erica said innocently, and then blushed. 'Oh—I'm not actually engaged to Sandy, you know, Mrs Dugall.'

'I beg your pardon, then. I distinctly got the impression—Ian, you are hopeless. I'm sure you said Erica was engaged to one of the senior doctors.'

'Practically engaged, I said, Momma dear.'

'I'm sure you said—— Oh well, never mind. Who did you say he was, Erica?' She broke off, and wrinkled her nose. 'Sandy, didn't you say? Isn't the Senior Registrar on your firm a man called Sandy Legrady, Ian?'

'Yes, that's the chap.'

'And Erica is——' Nancy gave a little frown. 'Isn't that rather an unusual situation?'

'Oh no, not in the least. There's no rule that says a girl can't be friendly with both a resident and a Registrar.'

'I'm sure in your father's day——'

'Etiquette isn't so strict now, even though Reidmouth *is* run on the formal Scottish pattern.'

'Even so, I'd have thought——' Then, seeing that the subject embarrassed Erica, Nancy dropped it.

Having got the weekend off, Ian had to make up for it for the rest of the week. As a result, Erica was with Nancy a great deal, showing her the sights and keeping her occupied. Ian hoped to be free on Friday night, and booked seats to take his mother to a play, but by Wednesday it became clear he wouldn't get off.

'David Hamilton's going home for the weekend and wants to travel Friday night,' he explained to Erica. 'The men on Mendelby's firm would help us out, only they're short-handed because of this strep. throat that's going the rounds. So it looks as if I'll have to stay in.'

'What a shame, Ian. You've only seen her in snips and snaps.'

'It's not for myself I mind, but Friday's her last evening in Dunedin—I did want to sort of give her a farewell "do".' He looked up hopefully. 'I suppose you couldn't go in my place?'

'Well, I——'

'Have you a date for Friday?'

'Not actually in so many words. I haven't seen much of Sandy this week, being out with your mother so much. But we generally go dancing on Friday evenings.'

'Look, if it's not actually settled, could you ask Sandy if he wouldn't mind? It's just this once, Erica.'

'I'd like to help out, Ian, but I have actually put Sandy off already this week——'

'Yes, but when this week's over things will be back to normal. Of course, if you'd rather not ask him——'

'I'll speak to him first chance I get tomorrow,' she said swiftly. She didn't like the faint hint that she was afraid to put off a date with Sandy. And after all, she told herself, just because we've gone out five Fridays in a row it doesn't mean we have to go out *every* Friday.

She found an opportunity soon after she came on duty on Thursday. 'About tomorrow night, Sandy——'

'Yes, where shall we go? The Waikopua, or that new roadhouse out towards Waitati?'

'That's what I wanted to say, Sandy. Would you mind very much if we didn't go dancing tomorrow?'

'What's wrong?' he asked with immediate concern. 'Feeling under the weather? This throat infection——'

'No, no, I'm fine. What I really meant was, would you mind if we didn't go out together? You see, Ian's mother——'

'Not again!' groaned Sandy.

'What did you say?'

'Last Saturday you couldn't get away in time for the theatre because you were having tea with Ian's mother. Last Sunday you couldn't come sailing although the weather was perfect, because Ian had hired a car to take you and his mother out for the day. Tuesday evening you were having dinner with her. Your afternoon off, you were taking her to a mannequin parade. And now you ask me to let her wreck our Friday evening!'

'Sandy, she'll be gone on Saturday. It was only common decency to prevent her from feeling lonely in a strange town——'

'Entertaining his mother is Ian's job.'

'But if he can't get off?'

'He should have thought of that before he let her come.'

'It was her own idea to come.'

'Then let her find her own amusement.'

'But Ian's booked these two seats for Friday. He meant it as a special occasion. Now he won't be able to go.'

'He's downright unlucky when he books seats, isn't he?'

'That's not a very friendly thing to say, Sandy!'

'I'm not feeling very friendly,' he retorted. 'That woman's absolutely monopolised you all week.'

'But it's just this one week, after all. And naturally I feel I must see as much of her as I can.'

'Why?' he said at once, pouncing like a barrister on the point he wanted to make. 'Why do you have to spend so much time with Mrs Dugall?'

'Well, I——'

'What's Mrs Dugall doing here in the first place?'

'She—she—— It's quite natural. She had a week to spare between engagements in Auckland. She wanted to see Ian and meet his colleagues——'

'Oh, quite,' he said with scorn. 'One brief conducted tour, ten minutes' chat with Galland, tea in the sitting-room, and that's that. Don't fool yourself, Erica. She came to Dunedin to meet *you*.'

'Partly that, of course. But——'

'Don't you realise you're being shown off to her like a prospective daughter-in-law? She came to have a look at the girl her precious son has fallen for——'

'No, no, Sandy, that's not so——'

'—And she's invited you on every possible occasion,' he pressed on, ignoring her interruption, 'because she wants to get to know you as well as possible before Ian commits himself. The son of the great Dr Dugall can't be allowed to throw himself away on just anyone. She wants to make sure you're attractive enough and well-educated enough——'

'You're quite wrong, she's not like that!' she said with indignation.

'You should know. You've spent enough time in her company. Well, she's had all the time I'm prepared to allow. You and I have a date for tomorrow and I intend to hold you to it.'

'We don't have a date,' she replied coldly.

'Of course we have. Every Friday we——'

'I don't remember making any such arrangement.'

'But it's understood between us——'

'If we're talking of "understanding",' she broke in, 'I'd have thought you'd understand that I want to keep Mrs Dugall company on her last night in Dunedin. She'll be all on her own, otherwise.'

'Then let her do something about it herself. She's encroached on you enough. Once and for all, Erica, I forbid you to go out with Mrs Dugall tomorrow evening.'

'You forbid me?' she echoed, on a note of disbelief.

He hesitated, but pride stiffened his determination. 'You have a date with me. I forbid you to break it.'

'I have no date with you. And if I had, I wouldn't let myself be held to it with chains and handcuffs.'

'There's no need to make a drama of it. I'm simply

telling you that that woman has got in our way enough.'

'In other words you're assuming the right to say who I can be friends with?'

'I think it's high time I did. I've had about as much as I can stand.'

Her chin came up. Her Scottish backbone stiffened. 'The remedy is simple.'

'Now look here——'

'I'm sorry, Sandy. I can't allow you to take charge of my life to that extent.'

'I've got to give way to every Tom, Dick and Harry you happen to feel sorry for? Is that it?'

'You speak as if there was a mob of people clamouring for my friendship. It happens to be one solitary woman on her own in a strange town. And I intend to help make her final evening in Dunedin a pleasant one.'

'Erica, I'll never forgive you if you do, after what I've said!'

'That's a risk I must take!'

'You mean you don't care? All right, that finishes everything. I've put up with your foolish notions about Ian Dugall because I hoped you might come to your senses in time. You'll have to choose.'

'I've told you—I won't let you run my life!'

Anger blazed in his grey-blue eyes like a fire behind ice. She tensed herself for the cruel things she could see struggling for utterance.

Then his broad shoulders sagged. 'I knew *he* would win,' he said wearily, and walked away.

The visit to the theatre was pleasant enough. When it was over Nancy said, 'Could you come to tea tomorrow before I leave for Auckland?'

'Wouldn't you rather have it on your own with Ian?'

'He can only get enough time off to come to the airport.

In any case, I'd like to have a chat with you, Erica.'

Rather apprehensively, Erica agreed. She was certain Nancy was going to ask if she and Ian were 'serious'—and she didn't know how to answer the question.

The hotel lounge was small and cosy. There was only one other occupant, an old man asleep over the *Otago Daily Times*. Nancy had tea brought to their quiet little corner, and warmed her hands on the side of the hot water jug.

'If it's like this in April, what will it be like in deep winter?' she murmured. 'I must send Ian's tweed overcoat as soon as I get back.'

'It does get cold here,' Erica admitted. 'We got some bad snow-storms last year in July and August. The town lies between the mountains and the ocean.'

Nancy poured the tea. A silence fell, the topic of the weather being exhausted.

'Was it about Ian that you wanted to speak to me?' Erica prompted, anxious not to prolong the ordeal.

Nancy flashed her a grateful smile. 'I suppose that goes without saying.' She fidgeted, then taking her courage in both hands said, 'You're genuinely fond of him, Erica, aren't you?'

'Yes, I am.'

'In a way, that makes it easier to say what I have to say. But in a way it makes it harder. You're not at all what I expected, Erica.'

'Why? What did you expect?'

'Someone harder and altogether more of a career-girl.'

'A career-girl? But how——?'

'When Ian used to write about you,' Nancy resumed quickly, 'it was easy to see he was very attracted to you. I hoped nothing would come of it—Ian takes a long time

85

to give his affections, as a rule. You were on the verge of becoming engaged to someone else, so he told me. But I thought perhaps you'd decided to switch to Ian because he was a better proposition.'

'Mrs Dugall, what are you saying?' Erica cried, her colour rising.

'I'm sorry, Erica. I know this must sound dreadful. I thought you were the kind of girl who was on the look-out for a husband who'd make good in the world. Oh, I've seen the type, my dear—both in the medical and the theatrical world. I thought you'd decided that Ian, with his innate ability and his great name to help him, was a better bargain than just any foot-of-the-ladder Registrar.'

Erica made as if to rise. 'I don't think we ought to go on with this——'

'No, wait, Erica. I've said I'm sorry. I wanted you to know what I had in my mind when I arrived. Well, no sooner did I see you than I knew I'd got it all wrong. I thought, "So long as they don't want to get married at once, it could work out fine." I won't deny that I've pictured Ian marrying someone who could bring him something more in the way of social standing or money—because, let's face it, these things count.'

'You've looked well ahead, Mrs Dugall,' Erica said rather coldly.

'Indeed I have. I've lived for the day when my son would be at the top of the ladder. But before that time, he's got to make good in his career. And it didn't take more than five minutes' conversation with Ian's colleagues to realise that he's not popular. And I didn't need much longer to work out why. It's because of you, Erica.'

'Because of *me*?' Erica stared at her, too astonished to say more.

'It's only natural they should side with Sandor Legrady.

He seemed a very nice man—the kind whose friends would rally round him. Naturally, they dislike Ian for breaking up his romance.'

'But you've got it all wrong——!'

'Dr Galland spoke quite well of Ian. It was the other men who seemed to have reservations. I was puzzled by the hostility I could sense. Well, you know I had a great deal of time on my hands, when both you and Ian were at work. I made it my business. . . .' Nancy flushed a little. 'The long and the short of it is, I've been going to a little place near the hospital for morning coffee, and getting to know some of the nurses. I didn't say who I was, I just encouraged them to talk. And I was really—really rather hurt and shocked about the things some of them said about my poor son.'

'Mrs Dugall, you shouldn't pay the slightest attention to hospital gossip——'

'But it must be founded on something, mustn't it? And the story as I pieced it together is that you and Dr Legrady were all set for a happy love affair, but Ian has spoiled everything. One little nurse even went so far as to—I didn't like her a bit. A little blonde girl.'

'Sally Goodrich?'

'I didn't get her name, but she's missed her vocation—she should be on the stage. But you must see, dear, that this sort of thing must harm Ian. If people are so set against him, his career will suffer.'

'Have you said any of this to Ian?'

'Of course not. It would never do to let him know I'm worried about him. I don't want to undermine his confidence in himself. But he has let slip one or two things about the work—things that have made me realise what a bad effect this antagonism is having upon him. He's no longer so sure of what he's doing.'

'Has it ever occurred to you——' She was going to ask if Nancy had ever wondered about the rightness of Ian's choice of career. But she remembered her promise not to speak of it, and fell silent.

'I can see he's worried and tensed-up,' Nancy said. 'He's tried to hide it, but you can't deceive a mother's eye, can you?'

'I suppose not,' Erica murmured. 'Well, what do you think should be done about it?'

'We-ell ... Erica dear, he hasn't known you so very long. He's very much attracted to you and I daresay if I asked him he'd say he was in love with you. But I know my own son. It takes longer than that for him to give his heart away. So perhaps it's not too late to prevent further damage. If you would help, I'm sure Ian's position at Reidmouth would be improved.'

'I'm not sure I understand.'

'His friendship with you is taking his mind off his work and antagonising his colleagues. Honestly, Erica, how can it be a good thing when Ian and his Registrar are rivals for the same girl? It must be terribly bad for both of them.'

'So what do you suggest?'

Nancy swallowed hard before answering.

'Erica, if you really care for Ian, you'll stop seeing him outside hospital hours and try to break off this disastrous friendship!'

Erica had thought this might be a difficult interview. So it was, but in a way quite different from her expectation.

'Do you really mean what you're saying, Mrs Dugall?' she asked, rather dazed. 'Are you so sure it would be for Ian's good if we stopped meeting each other?'

'The rest of the people he works with would stop blaming him for this unfortunate business with you and Dr Legrady. That must be for Ian's benefit.'

'But you know, he'd be entirely on his own without me. I'm the only friend he's got.'

'He'd make others, given time.'

'You really think so?'

'Of course I do. Ian always takes a while to make friends. I told you that. He'd probably have begun to form friendships at the hospital by now, except that— forgive me, my dear—you're in the way.'

Erica was about to reply, but stopped to think. Was it possible that Nancy was right? Surely Ian would have made at least some sort of contact with the others on the medical staff, if Erica hadn't monopolised him. Was she really doing what was best for him by allowing him to cling so exclusively to her? He himself had said 'I oughtn't to be having my hand held.' If he *had* to make friends, he would make the effort, perhaps. And when he left Reidmouth, what then? She wouldn't be there to help him. The time would have to come when he must manage without her.

Nancy saw that she had made Erica doubtful, and pressed her advantage. 'Ian thinks a lot of you, and you think a lot of him, I'm sure. I know it's painful to make a break like this. But if you really have his interests at heart you'll do it. Besides——'

'What?'

'If he really does fall deeply in love with you—and I don't rule that out—what happens then? You're not in love with him, you know. Do you think you are?'

'No-o——'

'Then isn't it best to make the break now, before it gets more difficult? Let him go, Erica. Clear his way for a new approach to the people he works with.'

'If I were really sure it was the right thing to do——'

'Give it a try, my dear. It isn't irrevocable. If you find I was wrong and things don't work out, you can always explain and take up your friendship again. Give it a try for two or three weeks, or a month. You could think of some excuse not to go out with him, couldn't you?'

'Yes, as a matter of fact ... there's a post in another department that rather attracts me. But I didn't want to leave the medical wards while Ian was there. If I got this new job, it would mean taking on extra work. I could easily be "too busy" to see Ian for the first few weeks.'

'Then that's perfect. You'll do it?'

Nodding, Erica picked up her bag and gloves and rose.

'You're not going?' Nancy said. 'You've hardly touched your tea.'

'In the circumstances, I think I'd rather leave now,' she said in a tired voice. 'Goodbye, Mrs Dugall.'

Nancy accompanied her to the hotel porch. 'I hope—I hope I've done the right thing,' she said uncertainly. 'You don't hold it against me?'

'Of course not.'

'You're a very sweet girl, Erica. Goodbye, and God bless you.'

The post for which Erica thought of applying had been advertised on the hospital staff noticeboard for some weeks now. None of the nurses had applied for it because, so the consensus of opinion went, 'it's an awful lot of extra work that isn't going to be much use afterwards when you apply for a new job.' Most nurses with an eye to the future like to have a list of special aptitudes and proficiencies which will impress an appointments panel; but the job which interested Erica was rather experimental, and might not be taken up by other hospitals.

The idea was to fit up a room in the hospital as a beauty salon. Here a trained hairdresser and beauty consultant would be available to attend the less ill patients who wanted a manicure or a set. This would be a tremendous boost to a woman's morale, especially a patient who had been in hospital for a long time. The more seriously ill cases, naturally, would need the services of a trained nurse; it would be unreasonable to expect a beauty consultant to deal with them.

Matron therefore wished the nurse undertaking this work to learn some of the techniques of beauty treatment. It was at this hurdle that most of the staff balked. 'What good will that do, if you go to a hospital where they don't run a scheme of this sort?' they asked each other. And the notice had stayed on the bulletin board, gradually getting dogeared.

Erica had always rather liked the idea. And now she saw in it a means of escape from Allerdyce Ward, from the two men who had pulled her life apart.

She put in her application that very Saturday afternoon, so that Matron should see it first thing Monday morning. As a result she was summoned to the office soon after the day's work began. Straightening her cap and tucking in the troublesome soft hair, she hurried off.

'Well, Nurse, so you think you'd like to train as a beauty consultant?' Miss Timms said with good humour. She was glad to have got an applicant at last; this was a pet scheme of hers.

'What exactly would it entail, Matron?'

'First of all, you would be transferred to Outpatients. You would work there on a half-time basis, and the rest of the time you would go to Miss Anville, the director of the Dunedin branch of Felicity Drew Ltd, for lessons in beauty care.'

'Yes, Matron.'

'To be perfectly candid, Nurse, if you're going to make

a success of this I think you'll have to give up quite a bit of your free time to practising these things. I daresay the other nurses will be quite glad to let you shampoo and set their hair or give them a manicure. I think this is one of those jobs where practice and experience will count for a great deal. Of course you're not expected to learn the whole hairdressing business from A. to Z.—that takes three years, I hear. But so long as you can cope with the simpler aspects of the work, that's all I want.'

'When should I begin, Miss Timms?'

'At once, unless there is any reason against it.'

'What about Allerdyce Ward, though?'

'As luck would have it, we think our advertisement for a Sister has at last brought us a suitable applicant, and if she can begin some time this week I can arrange for your ward to be covered for the next day or so, until she arrives.'

'Then you'd like me to make the change-over at once?'

'Yes, please, Nurse. You had better report to Out-patients Sister and ask where she wants you. The arrangement is that you should be on the morning clinics —let me see, that includes Orthopaedics, Psychiatric, Ophthalmic, so you have quite a range. I'll ring Miss Anville to let her know the scheme is at last under way. Is there anything else, Staff Nurse?'

'I don't think so, thank you, Matron.'

Miss Timms nodded and dropped her gaze to her memorandum book in search of Miss Anville's telephone number. But as Erica reached the door, she spoke.

'Staff Nurse Ryall——'

'Yes, Miss Timms?'

'I should just like to say that—in view of everything—I think you're making a very wise move in leaving Allerdyce Ward. I was about to arrange your transfer elsewhere myself. I don't think we need say any more, need we?'

Colouring deeply, Erica bowed her head in acknowledgment and hurried out. Was there anything, she wondered, that Miss Timms didn't know about her staff?

Now that she had taken the step, Erica was filled with a sense of relief. She would simply allow herself to be engulfed by the work, and stop worrying about everything else. She didn't allow herself to hear the nagging voice that said, 'You're not solving anything—you're just running away.'

She would be busy. So would Ian. She would keep out of his way, and soon he'd cease to think of her. Or at least—— But he *must* cease to think of her. He must learn to do without her.

As for Sandy—there was no need to avoid Sandy. The gap that had widened between them was more effective than physical absence. But it would be less painful if she didn't meet him. She still thought he had been wrong to speak to her as he did, and she couldn't bring herself to take the first step that might repair the damage. She had nothing to apologise for, she told herself firmly. Besides, it was better not to see either of them.

So she argued with herself. She took the first step towards freeing herself when she met Ian in Allerdyce Ward as she was collecting her belongings.

'Going? But where?'

'O.P.D. I've taken on that new therapy department. Half-time learning the beauty clinic business, and half-time in the hospital. I'm going to be pretty busy for a while, Ian. It means practising in my spare time.'

'I suppose you will,' he agreed, puzzled and a bit reproachful. 'You never said you were thinking of applying for this.'

'Didn't I? I've had the idea in mind for quite a while.'

'Seems an odd idea to me. Surely a hospital's for curing the sick, not giving hair-dos.'

'But if having her hair done helps a woman to get better faster?'

'That's just what Sandy said—almost his exact words.'

'Sandy?'

'Oh yes, he's in on this project—on the committee that recommended the idea. Sandy and the Lady Almoner and that chap in Psychiatric—they cooked it up between them. If you'd mentioned it to me, I could have told you.'

'With your mother in town, I haven't had time to discuss it with you.' This was a white lie, which he accepted without question.

'It's been pretty hectic for you, hasn't it? I do thank you for all you've done, Erica. And Mother sends her kind regards and her thanks. She particularly insisted I should say she sends her thanks.'

'That's all right. I was glad to have the chance of knowing her. Ian, I must go. Sister's waiting for me downstairs.'

'When do you think you'll have time for a little light relief?'

'I can't say for sure.'

'Well, look, ring me, will you?'

She forced herself to nod agreement, although she knew she wouldn't keep the promise.

It was he who rang her at last, eight days later. She said she was too tired to go out. Which was pretty well true. He rang again the following day. She sent Marion to answer the call with the message that she was busy, and couldn't come.

'He says not to forget you promised to ring him,' Marion reported.

'Thank you.'

'Will you ring him?'

Erica looked up from her work. She was setting Joanie Anderson's hair for her. Joanie said 'Ouch!' and Erica was saved the necessity of a reply.

'If you want my opinion, it looks as if you're giving him the brush-off,' said Marion. 'And if you are, you never did a more sensible thing in your life.'

'Yes, but look here, what happened to your romance with Sandy?' Joanie piped up.

'I told you two once before—you're a couple of old gossips. Hold still, Joanie—hang it, now I've got the roller tangled up in the back pin curls.' In remedying this muddle, their conversation was forgotten.

The last time Ian rang her, she took the call herself. She was on her way out to the Felicity Drew Salon to meet the beauty consultant who was to run the hospital salon.

'I can't stop now, Ian, someone's waiting for me at the salon.'

'In other words, you haven't got time.'

'I'm afraid not.'

'Shall I ring again, Erica?' he asked in a flat voice.

'Perhaps not for a week or two. I really am up to my eyes in work, Ian.'

'I see.' He hung up, without a word of farewell.

Biting her lip, she replaced the receiver and went on out of the Nurses' Home. She had done what she promised Nancy Dugall she would do. But whether it was right or wrong, she didn't know.

Before the hospital salon was put into commission, Matron asked for a meeting of the committee responsible for the idea. She asked Erica to attend with any criticisms and suggestions she might have.

Erica was nervous of being in a room with Sandy again. But as she listened to the talk go back and forth she forgot her nervousness, joined in with comments; soon the reserve between them had melted completely. In the eager discussion, there was even a sudden flash of agreement and understanding.

When the meeting broke up, Sandy detained her. They had both dealt with some of the women who were likely to be 'clients' in the beauty salon, and Sandy gave her the latest news on their condition.

The minutes went by unheeded. Suddenly he caught sight of his watch. 'My hat, look at the time!' He stood irresolute for a moment. 'I—I've enjoyed the committee meeting, Erica. It's been nice seeing you again.'

'It *was* interesting, wasn't it?' She made no direct reply to the second part of his remark, but her smile was answer enough.

'You—am I right in thinking you don't see much of——That's to say, you've had your shoulder pretty much to the wheel these past few weeks?'

'I've been very busy,' she agreed.

'How about giving yourself a break? I mean, just—just a meal somewhere?'

'Oh, I don't really know if——'

'No strings attached, Erica,' he said, almost in supplication. 'I'd just like to talk to you—to say something I've had on my mind for a long time.'

Without quite knowing what she did, she quickly put out a hand. He clasped it in his momentarily, a brief hard pressure.

'Oh, Erica,' he whispered, 'I've missed you so terribly.'

CHAPTER SIX

Erica was never sure afterwards whether she agreed in so many words to meet Sandy that evening at Cosimo's. But somehow it seemed a definite arrangement when she left him outside the committee room. And she found she was singing to herself as she took the blue silk dress from its hanger and let its smooth folds slip over her head. When she looked in the mirror, she was surprised at the girl who laughed back at her.

The familiar décor of the restaurant seemed to offer her an especial welcome. The soft light from the amber-shaded lamp touched her silk dress like rays from a setting sun.

'You look lovely, Erica,' Sandy said as he rose to greet her. 'I'm so glad you came. I was afraid you might decide against it.'

She met his glance with honest eyes. 'I'm not really quite sure why I did come,' she murmured.

'I wouldn't have blamed you if you'd decided I wasn't worth the bother.'

They waited until the waiter had taken their order. Then, very soberly and with a rather un-English formality, Sandy said, 'I ask your pardon for the way I behaved and the things I said. I had no right to interfere in your life. I've thought about it an awful lot and I can only say I was—I was too jealous to think straight. But that's no excuse. I'm deeply sorry. Say you forgive me, Erica.'

'I blame myself more than anyone,' she replied. 'It was

a difficult situation and I handled it all wrong.'

'I don't see how——'

'Oh, I let it drift on and on——'

'No one can accuse you of letting things drift now,' he said, concern in his eyes as he studied her. 'Warn me off if I'm rushing in where angels fear to tread, but is this a deliberate policy, this staying away from Ian?'

'Oh, is it—is it as obvious as all that?'

'Not to most people. When you moved to O.P.D. it was natural that you'd be busy with the new work, and a houseman is always busy, so it's quite natural that you wouldn't meet. But I have been wondering—was it because of anything *I* said?'

Her lips curved in a wry smile. She shook her head.

He looked both relieved and disappointed. 'I thought perhaps you'd realised you were walking along a path that would lead you straight down the aisle, and had decided you didn't want to marry Ian.'

'The last part at least is true,' she confessed. 'I don't want to marry Ian. I've never even thought about it.'

'You haven't? You don't feel like that about him?'

'I'm awfully fond of him——'

'Then why are you avoiding him? It's been three weeks now—I've been keeping count—and you haven't been out with him once.'

'I'd rather not explain, Sandy, except that his mother felt it would give him a chance to concentrate more on his work——'

'But it hasn't! Whatever gave her a soft idea like that? Surely it must be clear to her that if a chap loses the girl he loves, his work will suffer?'

'Ian isn't in love with me. Or at least, not seriously. It was just that he was lonely and worried, and I happened along. He'll get over it.'

'Is this his mother speaking, or you, Erica?'

'I'll leave you to guess which.'

'Whoever it is, I hope she's proved right. But Ian's taking a long way round to "get over it". The last few days he's been in quite a state.'

She bit her lip. 'But that will pass, Sandy.'

'Look here, I've been watching him——'

'But why? Why should you bother about him?'

'Oh well . . . I suppose it's the doctor in me. Or perhaps it's fellow-feeling—I could make a fair guess at what he's going through. Anyhow, I'd say he's very unhappy, and if his mother thinks that's helpful to him in his work, she's got very odd ideas.'

'Sandy, if you could do anything to help him—if you would try to help him over this bad time—I'd be so grateful!'

He sighed and shook his head. 'No one can help him. No one except you, that is.'

Throughout the meal they returned often to this topic. Erica was struck by how calmly Sandy could discuss the man he'd once dreaded as a rival; it was as if, after an exhausting struggle, he had regained a sane and balanced outlook. She said something of the kind to him and he gave his little shrug.

'I've had time to think, during the last three weeks or so. At first I managed to whip myself up into quite a hot rage about "the way you'd treated me" and so forth. But then—well, for one thing, I began to see that you were trying to make the break with Ian, and it began to dawn on me that my insane jealousy had probably been unfounded. It—it was a shattering realisation, Erica.' He rubbed his eyes momentarily. 'When I think how I'd got myself to the pitch when I almost hated the poor bloke——! And all the time what you were trying to tell me was the truth, that you just wanted to give him your friendship. I felt very, very small, my dear—so small that I'm surprised you can see me without a microscope.'

She laughed. 'It's nice to hear you talking like the Sandy Legrady I used to know.'

'The Sandy Legrady you used to know,' he replied seriously, 'is very anxious to put things back the way they used to be.'

There was a silence. Then Erica shook her head unwillingly.

'I don't think that's possible, Sandy.'

'Because of the way I behaved? But I've come to my senses now, Erica. And if you could forgive me——?'

'It's not that. It's not a change in you that makes it impossible, but a change in me.'

'I don't think I understand,' he said in dismay. 'Have I turned you so much against me?'

'No, no. Oh, Sandy—no, of course not. But you see. . . .' She broke off to gather her thoughts. 'Sandy, when you first asked me to go out with you a couple of months ago, I was thrilled to the core. I don't deny it—I was absolutely in the seventh heaven. But——'

'But I spoiled it all.'

'No, not that. Believe me, Sandy, this has nothing to do with what you said or did. The fault lies with me. I went into my romance with you convinced that it would be wonderful. I was simply infatuated—there's no other word for it. A silly, infatuated idiot!'

'Don't say things like that——'

'But it's true! I was flattered that you'd fallen for me. I was exultant to think I'd been able to do what no other girl at Reidmouth had done—I'd made a conquest of the most eligible bachelor in the town.'

'Oh, Erica, *don't*!' he groaned.

'It's dreadful when it's put into words, isn't it?' she said, her voice trembling. 'But you've been honest with me and I must do no less. Sandy, it was wrong of me—very wrong—to let you make love to me in the belief that I might return your feelings. Mine weren't genuine, like yours. Mine were a mixture of vanity and foolishness with only some real admiration to make a firm basis. I didn't find this out until afterwards. If I'd *really* cared for you my heart would have been broken when we quarrelled. If I'd *really* cared I'd have come to you and apologised——'

'You'd have been wrong to do that,' he put in like a flash. 'I was at fault, not you.'

'But I'd have *felt* it was all my fault. Instead I've been insisting to myself that I'd nothing to apologise for—and you know, that's not like a woman in love!'

'No,' he agreed slowly. 'No, I imagine that's true.' He moved his wineglass about, watching the pattern of light through the stem. 'But, Erica, I'm not asking you to be in love with me.'

'But you said——'

'I said I'd like to go back to the way things were before. That still stands. I always did say, didn't I, that your feelings for me were a lot less strong than mine for you.'

'Yes, but——'

'I always knew, at the back of my mind, that you hadn't fallen deeply in love with me. I just kept hoping that it would come. My mistake was in forcing the pace. But you see, I've never been in love before. And to tell the truth I'm fairly astonished at the way the disease has hit me! I always thought I was one of those men who had learnt to control his emotions. But I know myself a bit better now, and if you'd give me the chance I'd be less of a nuisance in the future.'

'I don't know,' she said doubtfully. 'Wouldn't it

be better not to——'

'It wouldn't be better for me! Seeing you this evening has been like coming to life again. Please, Erica—all I ask is your companionship now and again.'

For quite a while she went on expressing doubt. But like the arrangement to dine together that evening, the matter seemed to settle itself finally in Sandy's favour without any conscious decision on Erica's part.

She took care, though, not to let things run away with her this time. In the first place she really was extremely busy with the new job; and she continued to spend a great deal of her free time at the Felicity Drew Salon in the High Street, picking up hints on difficult beauty problems. Then in the back of her mind was the determination not to reawaken the hospital gossips. These had soon lost interest once Erica stepped out of the limelight, but she knew she only had to be seen a little too frequently with Sandy to have the hive buzzing again.

So out of every three or four invitations, she would accept only one. She went sailing one day of cold sunny weather, and found it exhilarating. She went to the hospital's autumn dance, but in a party that included four others besides herself and Sandy. And she went to a concert at Otago University. She noticed with some self-mockery that it worked out at about one date with Sandy per week. 'Like a Saturday treat,' she told herself. She didn't notice that the phrase implied how greatly she looked forward to each date.

Their fourth outing was a drive up into the hills to a local beauty spot on Sunday. The country around Dunedin was impressive in its early winter coat of nothafagus beech and dark brown ferns. On the summits of the high mountains to the west, the snow was gleaming proudly.

'Looks like a hard winter,' Sandy observed. 'My old friend from Beckybridge—remember him? Robb Tarryton?'

'The eczema case?'

'He was at my clinic the other day. He says these falls of snow in June mean heavier falls throughout July. "I'm stockin' up wi' tinned food and guid Scotch whisky," he said, "for fear we get cut off." '

'Has that happened since you've been at Reidmouth? That the hill farms have actually got cut off?'

'Only once in my four years. I remember it meant the devil of a lot of work for us—quite a lot of exposure and exhaustion cases, and one frostbite, not to mention the patients who'd got ordinary illnesses and couldn't be got out till the helicopters got through.'

He pulled up at the bridge on the Taieri River near a lovely little waterfall. They got out and walked on to the stone arch, leaned on the parapet to stare at the tumbling waters.

'Have you seen Ian recently?' Sandy asked. Alarm tensed the muscles round her mouth, but he hastened to reassure her with, 'It's all right, this isn't a jealous qualm—I know you haven't been meeting him. I meant literally—have you seen him, in the hospital?'

'Only in passing,' she replied. 'I'm right at the other end of the building now. And I don't have much contact with the medical ward, as you know.'

'When you've run across him, has he spoken to you?'

'No—he's usually seemed in a hurry and preoccupied. We certainly didn't stop and speak—and I didn't expect him to. Why do you ask?'

'I'm worried about him, Erica. He looks gaunt and miserable all the time, and he's so edgy——! Of course that's partly due to lack of sleep. We've had some urgent admissions at night recently due to this pneumococcus that's laying 'em low up at the hydro-electric scheme. He's had to be up and about when he ought to be getting some sleep. I've done my best to ease the load for him, but ... You know, he's said a couple of things recently that have really got me bothered.'

'What kind of things?' she asked, watching his face.

'The first was Friday, during the skin clinic. I told you Robb Tarryton was there. His case is pretty straight-forward, so I left him to Ian while I questioned a very interesting allergy case. I could hear a bit of a hoo-ha going on in Ian's cubicle, but I couldn't leave my own patient just then. Next thing I knew, old Robb was barg-ing through the ante-room, struggling into his jacket, as red in the face as the floor tiles. I nipped after him and grabbed him. He said Ian had been rude to him. It seems Ian—"that young de'il", he called him—couldn't get the hang of what he was saying—because of his accent, you know——'

'He does have a strong touch of Scots dialect in his speech,' Erica put in. 'Especially when he's excited.'

'That's quite true, but Ian shouldn't have lost patience with him. I had to tear him off a slight strip about it afterwards. Told him the patient-doctor relationship was terribly important—all that old guff, you know. Of course it's all quite true, but it sounds corny when you say so. Anyway, Ian said, "Never mind, you won't have to put up with me much longer." '

'I suppose he meant—he must have meant that he'll soon be moving on to a new job.'

'That's what I thought, and in any case we had a roomful of people waiting for us, so I left it. But then next day—that's to say, yesterday—we had a real shemozzle. We had a couple of pneumonia cases and a heart case.

Galland wrote them up for injections and told Ian to do the heart case while he and I did the others. That little blonde nurse——'

'Goodrich?'

'That's the one. She brought the hypodermics and the ampoules from Sister, who was at the drug cupboard. Ian took the ampoule she offered without a glance. God knows what made me walk up to look—sixth sense, maybe, or just pure chance.'

'You don't mean it was the wrong one?' Erica stammered, her voice full of horror.

'Ian nearly injected streptomycin instead of coramine. Erica, I didn't mean to show him up, before heaven I didn't. But I had to stop him.'

'Of course you had to!' She put her arm on his sleeve.

'Mind you, Nurse Goodrich was to blame initially. She didn't listen to what Sister told her. I wish somebody would tell that kid that quick wits and a talent for mimicry don't make up for carelessness—especially in a hospital ward.'

'She's been told a dozen times. I've tried to talk sense into her, and so has Marion. All the same, Ian should have checked.'

'Don't I know it? Galland let him have it, I can tell you. Galland's been getting a bit disillusioned about Ian lately, as it happens.'

'What did Ian do?'

'What could he do? He just had to stand there and take it. In fact, he seemed so dreary and subdued that when the old man had gone. I told him not to take it too much to heart. Ian said, "It doesn't matter. I've decided to give up the struggle." I don't know how to describe the way he said it. As if he were at the lowest possible ebb. It scared me, I tell you that. But you know him a lot better than I do. You don't think he meant anything—well, anything desperate?'

'Depends what you mean by "desperate". When he said he was going to give up the struggle, I think he meant the struggle to be a doctor.'

'Give up medicine? You're joking!'

'He's been on the verge of it for a long time.'

'Give it up? Ian Dugall's son? But why?'

'That's why, Sandy. Because he's Ian Dugall's son and he doesn't believe he can ever live up to it.'

'For Pete's sake——! He might give himself a chance! Nobody expects a first-year houseman to equal the names on the roll of honour! If he just pegs along like the rest of us, one day he'll make out all right.'

'He doesn't believe that. Listen, Sandy, I'm going to tell you something that nobody else knows except myself and Ian. You must never breathe a word to anyone— least of all to Ian.'

'I promise,' he replied, looking at her with grave grey-blue eyes.

'Ian's mother has made all sorts of sacrifices to get Ian through medical school. She wants him to carry on from where his father left off.'

'Yes, I quite see that, but——'

'Wait. The crux of the matter is, he's gone on with this plan because his mother has her heart set on it. But the poor boy feels he has no vocation as a doctor.'

'Oh, lord,' Sandy said in a low voice.

'Sandy, we both know that there are some doctors who are purely career men. Ian intended to be in that category. But beneath all that showy, self-important manner, he's desperately sensitive. He can't bear to fall short of what his father was. He hates himself for having no sympathy with the patients. I imagine that's why his brush with old Robb Tarryton upset him so much—it was another example of lack of contact between himself and the person he was supposed to help.'

'How did you find out all this?'

'That first day—you remember? The day you happened in on us shaking hands in the kitchen? I'd just helped him out of a scrape and he had given himself away—almost broke down. He'd never told a soul before that, although apparently he's been tortured by doubts since half-way through his student days. He's tried to make up in book-learning for what he lacks in instinctive understanding.'

'But he has it!' Sandy protested. 'I've seen it now and again—when he's stopped worrying about the impression he was making and concentrated on the patient. Not recently. Recently he's been a "go-by-the-book" man, and he's been worried and edgy when the book didn't tell him what to do. And of course he's been sharp with everybody. Erica, he's gone downhill since he lost your friendship. Could you tell me about that, or would you rather not?'

'I don't want to go into a lot of details. The long and the short of it is, his mother thought it would be for the best.'

'To cut him off from the only friend he had?'

'She didn't see it quite like that. She thought that as long as Ian and I remained close to each other, you'd—I mean, she thought——' She stammered into silence.

'You mean Ian's mother thought I'd have a down on him because he'd stolen my girl?'

'Well, she knew it wasn't exactly so black-and-white as that——'

'But in principle that's what she thought. She only met me for ten minutes. I must have made a vivid impression!'

'She doesn't know you as I do, my dear. And besides, there were other factors involved. Anyhow, she persuaded me that I ought to give Ian the opportunity to make other friends, and that's what I did.'

'And look what came of it. He's threatening to give up medicine. You don't really think he will, do you, Erica?'

Erica nodded emphatically so that her dark hair swung about her cheeks. 'Yes, I think he would.'

'It'd be an awful waste. I tell you, there's something there—if he'd only relax and let his own personality take over, there's the makings of a good physician in him.'

'But what's to be done to prevent him? Could you talk to him?'

'The chap he regards as his worst enemy?' Sandy shook his head. 'No, no.'

'Then what?'

'You could help him, Erica.'

She stared up at him. 'You mean—you want me to?'

'Yes, I do.'

'But that was the cause of all the trouble—it made you so miserable——'

'Things are different now. I understand the situation better.'

'Are you sure, Sandy? It might turn out to be a very difficult matter to handle.'

'It's difficult now—desperate, in fact. You can't leave the poor fellow to sink into failure. If he gives up medicine he'll regret it all his life. You *must* help him, Erica.'

She drew a deep breath, as if preparing to shoulder a burden.

'Yes, I must, mustn't I?'

'Why should you want to talk to me?' Ian said suspiciously.

Erica took a firmer grip of the telephone. 'Why not, Ian?'

'Why not? Six weeks—no, seven—seven weeks without a word except good morning as we pass in the corridors——!'

'I've been very busy, Ian——'

'But you had time to go out with Legrady!'

'Only a couple of times—and only in the last week or two.' This wasn't strictly true, but she wanted to minimise her meetings with Sandy. 'I've just come home from a drive to Beckybridge Falls with him, and we talked about you a bit, so I thought I'd ring you.'

'Talked about me?' His voice rose in anger. 'What's he been saying about me?'

'We can't talk on the telephone. Can't you come out for an hour or two this evening?'

'I could, but why should I?'

'Because there's something I'd like to explain.'

'Explain. . . .' He considered the word. 'I don't know that it interests me.'

'You'd rather just go on being angry with me, without hearing what I have to say?'

There was a pause. When he spoke again, the harshness had almost left his manner. He sounded uncertain and as if, against his will, he was finding something to hope for. 'I don't like being just picked up again when it happens to suit you, you know, Erica.'

'It isn't like that. Please meet me, Ian.'

'If you really have something you want to say. . . .'

'Then you'll come to the Barbecue coffee-bar?'

'I might be able to make it.'

'What time? Seven? Seven-thirty?'

'Seven-thirty. But I might be a bit late.'

'I'll be there.' She rang off quickly before his pride

could make him change his mind.

The idea of the interview to come filled her with nervous dread. She mustn't betray Ian's mother, so in talking to the son she could only tell half-truths. She must take all the blame of the separation upon herself. And in truth, the blame was hers. Knowing more about the situation than Nancy Dugall, Erica had let herself be talked into a course of action that she'd felt instinctively to be wrong.

When Ian came in, his black hair tousled by the onslaught of the night wind, she thought with concern, 'He looks almost ill!' She waved to attract his eye, for the place was crowded. He brought a cup of coffee across to the table, giving a great deal of attention to carrying it without spilling any.

'Hello,' she said. 'It's a wild night outside, isn't it?'

'Like everything else at Reidmouth, the weather is undependable.' There was a wealth of meaning behind the words.

'Ian——' She broke off. Across the narrow table another couple had ceased their conversation to listen to Ian's. Erica should have remembered how crowded this place became on a cold June evening.

'Drink up your drink and let's go for a stroll,' she suggested.

'I can't go far. I have to be in Furness Ward at eight-thirty.'

'We can walk to the park and back.'

He drained his cup and stood up to allow her to leave the booth. The cold wind buffeted them as they opened the café door.

'Hardly the night for a stroll,' Ian observed ironically.

'But we couldn't talk in there.'

'What are we supposed to talk about, anyway?'

'Sandy said this afternoon that you'd hinted you'd be

giving up medicine.'

'And how does that concern you?'

He wasn't going to make it easy for her. But then why should he? She clenched her fists in the pockets of her coat and sought for words with which to break through his resentment.

'I'm worried about you, Ian,' she said simply.

'Are you indeed? So worried that you've carefully kept out of my way for weeks on end! And don't tell me it was because you were so frightfully busy.'

'No, it wasn't entirely that,' she admitted. 'Although I have been busy, and tired at the end of the day.'

'Why did you do it, Erica?' he blurted out, turning suddenly to face her. 'Was it because Legrady didn't like our friendship?'

'No, Sandy had nothing to do with it. At least, not directly. But there was ill-feeling between you two, so I thought the best thing was to stop seeing either of you.'

'But you've been out with him!'

'Only very recently.'

'If it was all right to be friends again with him, why not with *me*?' he demanded jealously.

'Because—because I wanted you to make the effort to find other friends. I thought you were relying on me too much.'

'But that's what friends are for—to rely on! What good is it to promise to help and then snatch your hand away?'

'I know, Ian. I was wrong. I did it for the best, but I see now that I was wrong.'

'What's changed your mind?' he demanded with bitterness. 'Has Legrady been telling you what a first-class mess I've made?'

'He told me you were talking of resigning.'

'I've made up my mind to do it. I know at last that

I'm not cut out for a doctor.'

'Sandy says you are,' she replied briefly.

His head jerked round. 'He says I——? What makes him think so?'

'Experience, I suppose. He's seen a lot of housemen come and go in his four years here as S.M.R.'

'And he really says——?' Then, in the pale light from the streets lamps, she saw his lips curl. 'He can afford to talk like that—put on generous airs. It's always easy for the winner to be generous to the loser.'

'What makes you think that Sandy has won anything?' Erica asked, stifling her indignation.

'He's got *you*, hasn't he?'

'No, he hasn't, Ian, and please stop being so suspicious. I've told you what happened—now that I'm a bit less busy I've been out with Sandy on terms of simple friendship, and if you're willing you and I can be on the same footing. I've apologised for this long gap since last we had a talk—I've told you it was due to a wrong judgment on my part and I've said I'm sorry for it. What more can I say?'

'Do you really mean that there's nothing more than friendship between you and Legrady?' he persisted.

'Nothing more.'

'But how can that be? He's in love with you—always has been——'

'It's too long a story to go into now, Ian. The upshot was that I discovered my feelings didn't match with his and we agreed to be "just good friends", as they say in the gossip columns.'

Ian stood with his shoulders hunched, staring at the pavement. 'I don't know that I want to be "just good friends",' he said.

'Oh.' Erica was disappointed. She'd hoped that if she

accepted all the blame and apologised humbly, Ian would come half-way to meet her. 'I'm sorry,' she said. 'I hoped you'd find it in your heart to forgive me for letting you down.'

'It's not that,' he said swiftly. 'Don't you understand? Legrady may be able to play it cool, but I can't, Erica! I know now how much I need you—how lost and empty I feel without you. So far as I'm concerned, mere "friendship" is no use.'

'Oh, Ian!' she said despairingly. 'Ian, why must you make everything so horribly difficult for yourself?'

'I like to be honest. I may be a rotten doctor and as unpopular as the devil with my colleagues, but this virtue I can claim—I don't kid myself about anything. So let's give up this project, Erica. It's kind of you to try, but there's nothing you can do for me now. Just leave me to sink quietly, without trace.'

He turned and began to walk back in the direction of the hospital. Erica lunged after him and just managed to catch his sleeve.

'Wait, Ian—wait a minute! It's no good to——'

'I've got to go. I've a patient to check on.'

'Yes, but Ian——' She hurried along beside him, determined not to give up. 'Won't you just listen a minute?'

'What is there to say? I appreciate your offer, but I haven't Legrady's consolation of knowing you're already more than half in love with him. Now if you don't mind, I've got to rush back.' He shook her off and hurried away.

She stood alone, staring after him. She had failed.

Unable to face the prospect of talk and laughter in her quarters, she went for a walk. The wind pushed and pulled at her, like a living antagonist. She was tempted to go to

Sandy's flat. It would be a comfort to talk to him. But no, it wouldn't be wise. She had chosen the degree of their friendship and she must abide by that choice.

At length, driven by weariness, she went into a small café and had a meal. Afterwards there seemed nothing to do but go home.

On the message pad by the telephone in the hall she saw her name.

'Staff Nurse Ryall—please ring Dr Dugall.'

Unbelievingly she got the switchboard in the porter's lodge and asked to be put through to the telephone in the residents' quarters.

At the other end the receiver was picked up after the first ring.

'Could I speak to Dr Dugall, please?'

'Speaking. Erica?'

'Yes.'

'I'm an idiot, aren't I, Erica?'

She felt every nerve in her body relax. 'Well, yes,' she agreed, 'you are rather.'

'Is your offer still open?'

'Certainly.'

'Then—then I accept,' he said gratefully.

CHAPTER SEVEN

SHE'D imagined, when he rang her, that from now on it would be relatively plain sailing. And so it had seemed for the first few days. But then began the reproaches, the arguments, the accusations. . . .

'What did Legrady say when he was talking about me? I think he's got a nerve, discussing me with a third person! I suppose he thinks he put himself in a good light with you, acting the kind-hearted benefactor!'

Erica at first tried to defend Sandy's motives. But that only made matters worse. Time and again the conversation came back to the same point, or one very like it. She realised that the resentment Ian felt wasn't based on any one thing; as soon as she reasoned away one annoyance, another arose to take its place.

When she asked Sandy what he thought she ought to do, he sighed and shrugged. 'His way of looking at it probably goes like this: if she won't love me, it must be because she's already in love with *him*. So I'll show her what a mistake she's making by pointing out all his faults.'

'But he used not to be like this——'

'That was before he'd had the experience of struggling along on his own. Now he dreads the thought of losing you a second time, to the man he thinks you're going to marry.' Sandy smiled ruefully. 'I wouldn't mind so much if he were right on that point, at least. Poor old Ian . . . And poor Erica too. If I'd known he was going to prove so intractable I wouldn't have let you in for this.'

'But what am I to do?' she begged, hopelessly. 'Things can't go on like this!'

'Leave it to time and his own good sense. As time goes by he'll get back on an even keel. Don't let it get you down, darling. Come on now, cheer up.'

'I'm sorry.' She forced herself to smile. 'It's no use trying to help Ian if I'm all worried and woebegone myself, now is it?'

'That's the spirit. See here, how about letting me get tickets for the mid-winter Revue next week? That's always good for a laugh.'

'I'm going with Tom and Marion,' she told him. 'I was afraid both you and Ian would ask me—and as a matter of fact you both have! So I arranged to go with the love-birds.'

'Fine thing when you have to plan your life like an international conference!' he grumbled. But he accepted the decision with good grace.

The mid-winter Revue was a big event in the hospital's year. A joint effort by the medical and nursing staff, it was a chance for amateur talent; and it was surprising how much talent there was on the Reidmouth staff. They had the usual collection of magicians, comedians, tap-dancers, and ventriloquists. But in addition they had a house surgeon who could play like Semprini, a staff nurse who sang like Nancy Sinatra, and last but not least they had Sally Goodrich.

Sally was a newly-acquired asset to the revue writers. On the wards, Sister might frown at her inattention and the consultants look grave at her flightiness; but on the stage at the end of the dining-hall she was worth her weight in greasepaint. People who had eavesdropped on the rehearsals reported that she was screamingly funny in the sketches and even better when, on her own, she portrayed the hospital notables one after the other.

'I still think there's something a little bit cruel about the way she guys people,' Marion confided—a complete reversal of her previous opinion. Since the day she'd championed Goodrich, she'd suffered the probationer on her own ward and, moreover, caught her out mimicking her beloved Tom. 'All the same, there's no denying she's good at it.'

They were settling into their seats for the evening's entertainment. Tom was holding Marion's programme and her handbag and her box of sweets while she made herself comfortable. Erica, on her other side, was glancing round the hall. She saw Sandy's brown head overtopping the other men to whom he was chatting at the back of the hall. Ian was already seated at the end of a row near the door, these seats being reserved for those on call.

Matron came in, accompanied by the square figure of the Medical Superintendent, Dr Matthewes, and his wife. Just behind her stalked Sir Vian Partick, Chairman of the Management Committee. Other, lesser celebrities brought up the rear. This was a sign that the lights would now be dimmed. Sandy and his friends came down the gangway, looking for seats. Erica noticed Ian watch narrowly to see if Sandy would sit near her. But luckily the group found places together in a row on the other side of the gangway.

The quartet began the overture. The red serge curtains parted to reveal a row of pretty young nurses in Floradora dresses who assured their audience that they were plain old-fashioned girls offering "Plain Old-Fashioned Fun". This was the title of this year's revue, and once having established that fact the girls brought on the 'stars' one by one.

The first half ran its course. Some of it was very witty, some of it was very bright, and some, inevitably, had been seen before. Hospital foibles were noted, hospital grouses were aired, some well-known hospital personalities were reminded of their failings, and some hoary old jokes were revived yet again, to groans from the audience.

'The sketches are the best,' Erica said. 'They always are, but this year they seem even better. That one about Miss Chatworth's gardening efforts——!' (Miss Chatworth was the Night Superintendent, who kept trying to grow plants in pots which inevitably got knocked over, walked into, or dropped.)

'It wouldn't have been so funny except for Nurse Goodrich,' Tom put in. 'She's so like Chattie in her gardening gloves, it makes you blink.'

The telephone could be heard ringing in the dining room supervisor's office.

'Bet you what you like that's for me,' Tom said gloomily. 'I ought to be on the end of the row, you know, Marion.'

But the porter who had taken the call disappeared through the door leading backstage. And before the second half of the revue opened, the compère came before the curtains.

'As you may have guessed, one of our cast has just been called away. This means that the next item will not be the sketch "Have it Your Own Way", but will be item No. 14—"Dancing Feet". We hope to include the sketch later in the revue if Mr Pelton gets back. Thank you.'

The programme having been disorganised, there were some long, long waits and much scurrying about behind the scenes between the items. The audience were accustomed to these mishaps and bore with them patiently. But at one point the wait became very lengthy indeed. The compère reappeared.

'Ladies and gentlemen, there's been a mishap——'

(groans)—'because of the costume changes getting out of order. We need a little time to get organised. So to fill the gap——' (cheers)—'our clever little Sally Goodrich has agreed to come to our rescue with a party piece that, so her friends tell me, is "simply fabulous". Ladies and gentlemen—pretty, witty Sally Goodrich!' (Prolonged cheers and applause.)

The curtains parted. A chaise-longue stood on the stage, on which reclined a figure covered by a pink nylon sheet. This figure, on closer examination, proved to be made from two bolsters and a wig. The audience waited, mystified.

On came a small figure in a staff nurse's uniform. She was carrying a shallow oblong tray of pink plastic. She set this down on a table alongside the recumbent figure and said brightly, 'Good morning, Mrs Hourglass. All ready to have your face lifted?'

The audience exploded in mirth. Heads turned towards Erica.

'Why, it's me!' she exclaimed, laughing.

Sally was busy taking out the tools of her trade from the plastic tray. They weren't the usual exaggerations of hospital revue, where surgeons tend to be armed with hatchets and cutlasses. Instead it looked as if she had brought on stage the contents of her theatrical make-up box, and these she now proceeded to recommend to her 'patient'. Having talked the unlucky Mrs Hourglass into having the shape of her eyebrows entirely altered, Sally got on with this task, chatting brightly to distract the patient's attention from the dire results.

Needless to say, Erica had never attempted anything of the kind with any of her patients and everyone in the audience knew it. But it was undeniably funny to hear 'herself' getting into a panic as first the left eyebrow and then the right was altered and yet never matched.

'It's like when you try to shorten the leg of a wobbly table,' she gasped to Marion between gusts of laughter.

But then, almost immediately, it began to be less amusing for Erica.

'Of course your husband will like it,' Sally was assuring her hapless victim. 'It's no use telling *me* he's a difficult man. All men are difficult, and some are downright impossible, as who should know better than me? But I know all about handling difficult men. I make quite a hobby of it. Ask anyone in the hospital and they'll tell you Staff Nurse Tryall is so expert she can handle two difficult men at once. Yes, really—I mean it! Of course I do it from the very noblest motives, you know. I'm not a bit influenced by the fact that one of them is obviously on his way to the top and the other has a name worth a hatful of gold.'

Erica had felt herself going hot as this speech proceeded. She was almost glad of the interruption caused by a sudden hubbub on the opposite side of the hall. She turned her head, and even in the dimness could see that Ian had got to his feet noisily. For one terrible moment she thought he was going to make a public protest; but instead he walked to the door, thrust through it angrily, and went out leaving it banging to and fro on its spring.

Nurse Goodrich, distracted by the noise, had paused. A polite little outburst of applause prevented her from resuming.

'Jolly good,' said Sandy's voice in calm approval. 'Very good. Give the little lady a big hand.'

Relieved to be shown a way out of their embarrassment, the friends sitting with Sandy applauded loudly. The rest of the audience followed suit. Although clearly there should have been more to come, Sally made her bow and, looking nonplussed, went off. The curtains closed and the quartet struck up for the next item, drowning the babble of disapproving comment over what had just happened.

Erica pushed past the other people in her row. Sandy joined her as she made for the door.

'Did you see his face?'

'Oh, Sandy, how are we going to smooth *this* over? What a ghastly thing to happen!'

'I'll wring that kid's neck for her in the morning——'

'I wish she'd learn to curb her tongue! I know she was pushed on-stage at short notice to keep us occupied, but all the same——!' They were out in the main corridor now. 'Where would Ian go?'

'Doctors' sitting room? No, he might run into other people there. Perhaps the wards—no, there he is!'

He was just disappearing through the side door to the Inner Quadrangle.

'Going out, the silly chump. He's not allowed—he's on duty.' He shouted, and Ian wheeled.

He would have gone on his way, but the sight of Erica hurrying up behind Sandy made him pause. The open door still in his hand, he waited. The south wind from the Pacific flapped the edge of his white coat, and blew Erica's hair in strands across her face. In the corridor it made a faint moaning sound.

'What do you want?' Ian said shortly.

'You're not thinking of going out, are you?'

'What business is it of yours?'

'Ian, don't let it bother you,' Erica began in a rush. 'What Goodrich said, I mean. It's not worth getting upset——'

'Who's upset?' he asked with a crooked smile. 'I absolutely adore being held up to public ridicule. I thought it was tremendous fun.'

'Matron will have something to say to Nurse Goodrich,

I should think,' Sandy put in. 'You can rely on her to take care of it.'

'Oh, really? You think that a few sharp words from Matron will blot tonight's performance from everyone's mind?'

'Oh, don't be silly, Ian. Everyone knew it was nonsense.'

'That's very comforting. You seem to have forgotten that she's been doing that as a "party piece" for some time and that her friends think it's "simply fabulous"—at least so we were all told. Maybe you don't mind that sort of thing, Legrady, but I do.'

'I can't say I exactly enjoy it, but I've got more sense than to make it worse by publicly walking out——'

'What do you think I should have done? Sat there quietly and let her go on dissecting my private life in front of the whole staff?'

'Look here, Dugall, it's no use getting huffy with me about it. I was as much at Goodrich's mercy as you were, and——'

'But I notice you just sat there like a tame rabbit and let her say what she liked! I at least had the courage to walk out in protest.'

'Before you interrupted, I was saying that I was at Goodrich's mercy—and so was Erica. You were the only one who ran away from it.'

'Ran away?' Ian flashed. 'I notice you weren't far behind me once I'd led the way.'

'Nurse Goodrich's performance is over, otherwise I'd still be there facing it out.'

'That's only another way of saying you'd have let her do what she liked without contradiction. Well, I have more respect for Erica's feelings and my own to——'

'Erica's feelings? You really think you made things

better for Erica by staging a public walk-out? Stop fooling yourself, Dugall.'

'Please—please——' Erica begged. 'Sandy, please don't take that tone with him!'

'It's all right, Erica, let him say what he likes,' Ian said coldly. 'He can't make any difference to the facts, and the facts are that I wasn't willing to let you be made a laughing stock.'

'Grow up!' Sandy exclaimed. 'You're trying to justify what you did by claiming it was all for Erica's sake. But the truth is you just couldn't stand it and you ran away—and by doing so drew everybody's attention to yourself and made it ten times more embarrassing for us.'

'That's not so! You don't think that, Erica, do you?'

'No, of course not——'

'I knew you'd understand——'

'What did you expect her to say?' Sandy demanded. 'You know darn well that Erica would do or say anything to keep you happy——'

'And how you hate the thought!' Ian said in triumph. 'It rankles with you, doesn't it, that she cares about me? You thought that by this time you'd have established an exclusive authority over her. Oh, I haven't forgotten how miserable you made her with your possessive attitude!'

'Dugall, I came after you with the intention of helping——'

'Helping? You really want to help? I'll tell you how!' Ian's voice was thick with dislike and resentment; he scarcely knew what he was saying. 'Just leave us alone, that's all. Leave Erica alone to lead her own life instead of domineering over her, and stop interfering between us——'

'Ian, you're talking nonsense. Sandy isn't interfering——'

123

'But I say he is, Erica. He's the kind of fellow that wants to manage everyone's life for them, and to make sure that he's top dog. You told me yourself that he'd never have noticed you except that you'd taken the trouble to make friends with me. He's the kind of fellow that wants what someone else has got——'

'That's simply not true, Ian——'

'You're too kind-hearted to see him in his true light, Erica. He expects everyone to come running if he crooks a finger. Can't you understand that he'll go on trying to reduce you to the level of all his other inferiors? We've got to face up to him——'

'No, no, you're wrong, Ian. Sandy has tried to help you——'

'Oh yes, I can just imagine the yarn you've heard from him. Big-hearted, noble, charming Dr Legrady, friend to all the junior members of the staff. Did he tell you how he showed me up in front of Galland a couple of weeks ago?'

'But you must admit he *had* to stop you when you were on the verge of giving the wrong injection——'

'Ah, so he did tell you! I might have known he wouldn't miss a chance to show you what a fool I am——'

Sandy said something under his breath in forceful Hungarian. Aloud, he said, 'I told her about it because I was trying to explain what a mess you were getting in these days——'

'Kind of you!'

'Hang it, man, don't turn everything I say inside out! I *did* mean it kindly. And the proof is that I persuaded Erica to get on friendly terms with you again, because you needed someone to turn to.'

'That's not true,' Ian said harshly. 'Erica wouldn't need instructions from you. She came back to me because she loves me.'

'I didn't say I gave her instructions. You're determined to twist my words. All right, I'll give it to you straight— you don't know when you're lucky, Dugall! Erica has wrestled with your self-pity and your moodiness until she's nearly exhausted. I blame myself for talking her into it. All it's done is make her miserable. Pull yourself together, for Pete's sake, or the next bit of "interfering" I'll do is to persuade her to drop you again.'

Ian stared at Sandy, and what he saw in that austerely angry face made him hesitate. His determination to discount anything Sandy said began to crumble. He turned horror-stricken eyes on Erica.

'You mean he *told* you to ring me?'

'No, of course not, Ian——'

'He had nothing to do with it, had he!' he cried, in vast relief. 'I knew he was lying.'

'Ian, stop hating him for every word he utters. He did try to help you. He really did.'

'But you would have telephoned me whether he spoke to you about me or not. You would, wouldn't you, Erica?'

'I—listen, Ian——'

'No, answer yes or no. If Legrady hadn't "talked you into it", you wouldn't have contacted me?'

'We—we discussed it. I told you so at the time. I did, Ian—remember?'

'Yes,' he said slowly, 'but you didn't tell me I only came back into your life on sufferance.'

With a swift movement he suddenly pulled the door open and walked out. They could hear his hurrying footsteps recede on the concrete path towards the main drive.

Sandy rubbed his mouth. 'Heaven forgive me,' he said in a shocked voice. 'Now what have I done?'

CHAPTER EIGHT

MATRON arranged the papers on her desk for a moment, then looked up again.

'Am I to understand, Nurse, that you actually saw Dr Dugall leave the premises?'

'Not—not exactly, Matron. I saw him go out the side door that gives on to the path round the Quad. I don't know that he actually went out. He was wearing his white jacket.'

'He left that in the porter's lodge. You know that most of the residents keep a raincoat or something of the sort in the little alcove at the side of the reception desk. His coat is gone. Unfortunately Tubalt had slipped into the main building to look at the revue—most wrong of him to leave his switchboard, but there it is. It really seems incontrovertible that Dr Dugall went out.'

'I suppose so. . . .'

'I may as well tell you that this isn't an inquiry into a minor dereliction of duty. If it were only that Dr Dugall left the premises without telling anyone while he was "on call", it would be a small thing compared with this.'

'Why? What's happened?' Erica's throat was unbearably dry. 'Oh, Matron, what's he done?'

'He's gone, my dear. His bed hasn't been slept in. As far as we can make out, he left the building after that disgraceful performance by Nurse Goodrich, and hasn't been back.'

'Oh——! Miss Timms!' Erica felt the blood rush from

her face, and knew how she must look from the alarm in Matron's eyes.

'Sit down—sit down, Staff Nurse. I'm sorry if this is totally unexpected. To tell the truth, I thought you might know what had happened.'

'I knew he had gone out. I thought—I thought, perhaps, he'd gone out for a drink. Of course I knew he oughtn't. But Dr Legrady——'

'Quite. Dr Legrady arranged for Dr Hamilton to cover for him. Yes, Dr Legrady told us this morning. He's told the Medical Superintendent more or less what you've told me. But, to be perfectly frank, Dr Matthewes and I hoped you might have heard from Dr Dugall since he left the hospital.'

'No, Matron. Not a word. I'd no idea he'd not come back.'

Matron's cool discipline deserted her for a moment. 'Where can the silly young man have gone?' she demanded irritably, drumming the desk with her fingers. Then, catching sight of Erica's unhappy face, she recollected herself. 'I'm sorry, my dear. I realise this is a worrying situation for you. Have you *any* idea where Dr Dugall might be?'

'Have you tried his home address—with his mother in Auckland? He might have caught a plane. . . .'

'Naturally we thought of that first. Dr Matthewes' secretary has been trying the number all morning, but there's no reply.'

'That doesn't necessarily mean he's not there. His mother may be at the studios or somewhere, and if Ian— Dr Dugall—is there alone he may simply not be bothering to answer the phone.'

'I needn't tell you, Nurse, how extremely serious this could be for Dr Dugall. If his absence goes on, Dr Matthewes may have to consider his contract broken. On the other hand, if he were persuaded to come back at once, or at least write pleading indisposition or something of the sort, a lenient view might be taken. Especially in view of Nurse Goodrich's cabaret turn last night.'

'If it hadn't been for that——!' Erica burst out. 'How could she do such a thing?'

'I wondered that at the time, and I asked her that very question this morning. Naturally we all expect to see a good deal of leg-pulling in the mid-winter Revue, but only public reputations may be attacked. Our private lives have always been respected—except in unusual circumstances when for reasons of discipline official action has to be taken. I explained that to Nurse Goodrich and you can expect a full apology from her. She has already apologised to Dr Legrady.'

'It doesn't matter about an apology,' Erica said impatiently, quite forgetting she was speaking to Matron.

'Well, yes—apologies aren't going to remedy the damage,' sighed Miss Timms regretfully. 'Dr Dugall has really put the cat among the pigeons, hasn't he?' She paused and when she resumed it was in an informal, almost motherly tone. 'I may as well admit that a good deal of the story is common knowledge. You remember that when you asked to be transferred from Allerdyce Ward I mentioned that I thought it was a good move. Unfortunately, it didn't have the good effect I hoped for. I watched with some interest when you renewed your friendship with him. I decided not to say anything because, to tell the truth, I thought it could only be beneficial—I thought he might get the better of this phase of restless moodiness with your help.' She sighed. 'I was a nurse at St Gregory's when his father was there,' she added. 'He was a very great man, and for the sake of his memory we all want to do what we can for the son.'

'Matron, do you think it would do any good if I flew up to Auckland?' asked Erica all at once.

'Today, you mean?'

'It's my weekend off; I could catch the afternoon flight.'

Miss Timms looked thoughtful. 'Well, as a matter of fact,' she said at length, 'I can't think of anyone who'd have a better chance of making him see reason. Whether you go or not depends entirely on your own wishes because, as I told you, private affairs are outside official province. But I must admit it would give us at least some hope of repairing the damage.'

Erica went in search of Sandy to tell him her plan. He would be in Men's Medical, but he'd be busy because on a Saturday Dr Galland didn't come. She left word with Marion.

He came to the office in O.P.D. about an hour later. 'I couldn't get away earlier. Having to go to the Superintendent's office has put me behindhand. And of course, no houseman on our firm and no consultant this morning. You've heard he's vanished, I suppose?'

'Yes, Matron sent for me and told me. They thought I might have news of him.'

'But he hasn't been in touch?'

She shook her head. Sandy drove his fist into the palm of his other hand.

'My fault,' he groaned. 'And I was the bloke who was supposed to be trying to help him!'

'It's not your fault, Sandy. Who could ever have guessed he'd do something so irresponsible?'

'Have you any idea where he might be?'

'I think he's at home. I'm going to Auckland on the afternoon plane from Momona to try and talk some sense into him. Matron agrees it's a good plan.'

'I hope you have success. Otherwise. . . .'

'You couldn't come with me, I suppose?'

'I wish I could, but we've still got these pneumonia cases coming in from the hydro-electric scheme at Roxburgh, and we're so short-handed. I daren't go.'

'No, of course not.'

'I'll try to get away to see you off.' He pressed her hand and hurried back to his work.

He was nearly too late at the airport. A light covering of hoar frost edged the runways. He folded Erica's coat collar close against her neck with gentle hands.

'Here comes the bad July weather Robb Tarryton promised us,' he said. 'Take care not to catch cold. And ring me as soon as you've got any news.'

'You'll be at the hospital?'

'Yes, I'll sleep in over the weekend, I think—in case we get any more emergency cases.'

'I'll bring Ian back so he can take over his share of the job,' she said, attempting lightness.

'You wouldn't have to go off on this jaunt if it weren't for my clumsiness last night. I could kick myself——'

'If it hadn't been that, Sandy, it would have been something else,' she murmured. 'He was at breaking point. That's all there is to it.'

The loudspeakers called the flight. Sandy gave Erica a quick kiss and watched her join the departure group.

The journey was uneventful. Erica took a taxi straight from the airport. The driver had some trouble finding the place, which proved to be a little block of flats behind a row of shops in Auckland's North Shore area—and who should be stepping out of a taxi at the entrance to the block but Nancy Dugall.

'Mrs Dugall!' called Erica, thrusting money at her driver and running after her.

Nancy stopped with her key half-way out of her hand-bag.

'Erica! What are you doing here?' Her glance went to Erica's taxi, as if expecting someone else to be there. 'Is Ian with you?'

'No—I thought—didn't he come home last night?'

'Last night? But he hadn't any leave——?'

'What time did you go out this morning?'

'Early. I had to be at rehearsal by eight. Why?'

'He may have arrived after you left. Can we go up and see?'

Nancy hastily led the way inside. As the bright yellow door swung open she called 'Ian? Ian?' but there was no reply.

They hurried through the rooms but the little flat was quite empty, with the remains of Nancy's hasty breakfast still on a tray in the living room.

Nancy sat down, pulling off her hat. 'Why should he be here?' she asked. And then, accusingly, 'What have you done to my son?'

'Can you think of anywhere he might have gone?' begged Erica. 'Any relative, any friend?'

Nancy gave her a keen glance, then shook her head. 'If he were in any trouble, Ian would come to me. And he is in trouble, isn't he?'

'I'm afraid so, Mrs Dugall. He's left the hospital without permission. We've got to get hold of him and persuade him to go back——'

'But where is he? Where can he be? If he was worried or unhappy, why didn't he come to *me*?'

'I don't know.' Erica thought it over for a while. 'If he had shown up here last night, what would you have done?'

'Sent him back, of course, as soon as I discovered he

had left against orders.'

'That's why he didn't come here,' she murmured. 'I should have realised that. He knew you would force him to go back.'

'But I don't understand—*why* has he done this?'

'There was a piece in the hospital revue last night—it upset him and then—I tried to calm him down—Oh, it's too difficult to explain.'

'I knew he'd taken up with you again,' Nancy said slowly. 'His letters have been full of you again. I can't help thinking his friendship with you has been a misfortune. You mean well, I know—but you don't know how to handle him.'

'And you think you do?' Erica queried sadly.

'Of course I do. I'm his mother.'

'But he didn't come here last night. He didn't want to face your arguments.'

'What are you saying? Ian's not a fool—he knows he's got to go back to Reidmouth——'

'I think maybe he's made up his mind not to.'

'But that's absurd. That's as good as saying he's made up his mind to throw up his career.'

'Yes, that's what I mean.'

'Nonsense! Why, a career in medicine has been his life's ambition!'

'I know it sounds incredible to you. We'd better not talk about it. If you'll just try to think where he might have gone——'

'But we must talk about it. Erica, you don't really mean he's threatened to resign?'

'I don't know if I ought—— Oh, you'll have to know now,' she cried in despair. 'Yes, he's been miserably unhappy. He's felt for a long time that he made a wrong choice——'

'But you're wrong! He's never had any doubts!'

'None that he's confided to you, Mrs Dugall. He didn't want to hurt you. He knew you had your heart set on seeing him a successful man of medicine. He's hidden his doubts from you. And from everyone else too, by assuming an air of self-importance——'

'What are you talking about?' cried Nancy, incredulous. 'Ian's not self-important! If anything, he's too shy and quiet.'

'So he is, underneath. But the face he shows to the world is a bold, self-confident face. *That* was why he was so unpopular at Reidmouth. It had nothing to do with rivalry between him and Sandy.'

'You must be mistaken——!'

'Mrs Dugall, I don't claim to know every side of this business, but this much I do know—Ian was and still is unpopular with the staff at Reidmouth because of his cocksure manner. I know this is true, because I disliked him myself until I found out what he was really like. After that happened, he and I grew rather close. And that was why he told me about his doubts.'

'He told you. Yet he never told me. His own mother . . .'

'You honestly never suspected he was worried?'

'Never!' she cried. 'Never! And why should he be worried? He's clever and capable, and has his father's name——'

'But no vocation,' Erica put in quietly.

'How dare you say that!'

'It's true, Mrs Dugall—or at least Ian thinks it is. And that's why, when you get down to fundamentals, he's run away. It's not really because he was held up to ridicule or because he felt I didn't love him enough. If he'd had his work to turn to, neither of those things would have had the power to make him go. But he's got nothing—no friends, no purpose in life. And so he's thrown in his hand and run away.'

Nancy, stricken to the heart, stood up and turned away. She hid her face in her hands. 'But I only wanted him to be happy,' she said brokenly. 'I thought it was what he wanted—to tread the path his father trod. Oh, my poor boy, my poor boy—what have I done to you?'

'Don't cry, Mrs Dugall. If we can get him back——'

'But where has he gone? What's happened to him? Oh, if I hadn't failed him so terribly, he would have come to me and told me what was wrong, and I could have helped him. God forgive me, God forgive me, I've failed my own son!'

Erica put an arm round her and drew her close. She stroked the lovely ash-grey hair. 'We'll find him. I promise we'll find him. Everything will be all right. If he doesn't want to go on with his career in medicine, it's not the end of the world——'

'No,' exclaimed Nancy, looking up through her tears, 'no, he can do anything he wants! We must find him and tell him——'

'So dry your eyes and think of all the people he knows—school friends, men from his medical school.'

'But he has no real friends,' Nancy confessed. At her own words she looked shocked. 'Where can he have gone, Erica? You don't think we—we ought to call in the police?'

'No, no, we've scarcely begun to look. We've no reason to think he's come to any harm——'

She broke off. The thought that had been haunting her since this morning suddenly leapt to the front of her mind. In the state of mind he'd been in, Ian might have done anything.

Then she took a hold on herself. The Medical

Superintendent had been on the telephone most of the morning and there wasn't the slightest doubt he'd already contacted all the hospitals in the area. If Ian had come to any harm, they would know it by now.

'You know, the more I think of it, the more I think he must be still in Dunedin,' she burst out. 'He walked out without taking any of his belongings. He probably only had the money that was in his pockets. Oh, what a fool I am—why didn't I think of that before? He hadn't the funds to get far! Ten to one he's still in Dunedin somewhere.'

When she rang Sandy, she suggested this to him.

'Right. I can get out for part of the evening. I'll go round the hotels and things. What about you, Erica? Are you coming back?'

'Mrs Dugall's asked me to stay the night, but I'll take the first plane in the morning.'

'I shan't be able to meet you, I'm afraid. They're getting a replacement for Ian from the Public Hospital, but he doesn't start with us until Monday. So I'm staying on duty.'

'I'll come in and have lunch in the dining hall. I'll see you then.'

The journey back took much longer than the trip north. The farther south they travelled, the more snow clouds closed down visibility. She arrived in Dunedin two hours late.

She went to the hospital and had a word with Sandy. He had nothing to report. His inquiries among the hotels and boarding houses had yielded no results.

'Where else could we try?' she begged.

'We could try widening our field—take in more of the outskirts of Dunedin. One thing's sure—if only he had the money in his pockets, he'll soon run short. Of course,'

Sandy added, sighing, 'he may take a job.'

'Sandy! You don't think—you don't think he'd take a job on a ship? There have been several sailings from the docks since Friday night.'

He ran his fingers through his hair. 'God knows,' he muttered. 'God knows.'

The wintry spell continued. Reidmouth Hospital had to reorganise its resources to cope with the influx of acute bronchitis and pneumonia cases, and as traffic became snarled up on the icy roads in the mountains there were a number of casualties. Erica was loaned to Casualty to help deal with the increase of work, and was glad of it. She needed to be kept busy as Monday passed, and then Tuesday, and still no news of Ian.

On Tuesday afternoon, just as she was going off duty, a bus skidded on the frosty crossroads out of the town. No one was seriously hurt, but there were cuts and bruises. An ambulance brought these patients to the hospital, and who should Erica see among them but old Robb Tarryton.

'Hello, Mr Tarryton. Remember me?'

'Why, it's Nurse Ryall that used to be in Furness Ward. How are you, Nurse?'

'Quite well, thank you. You've been in the wars, though. Mr Quillan will stitch that gash in a minute. Like a cup of tea while you wait?'

'Ah, that I would,' he replied with a wily glance from faded blue eyes. And when she brought it he said triumphantly, ' 'Tis the second cup I've had out of the hospital today!'

'The second cup?'

'I had a cup in Outpatients this afternoon. That's why I was on the bus—goin' home after Outpatients. Fix me up quick, there's a good lass, so I can get off home before the snow comes on again up in Manuka Gorge.'

'It's going to snow again, is it? Does you rheumatism tell you that?'

'Don't need rheumatism to know that those clouds s'afternoon had a load to drop.'

Presently the cut was stitched and he was allowed to go.

'Will you be all right?' Erica said. 'Shall I see you to the bus depot? I'm going off duty and I could come down the road with you.'

'Would you do that? I'd appreciate it, Nurse. Not as steady on my pins as I'd like, these days.'

Erica put on her cloak and accompanied him.

'Ah, this is what I call service,' Mr Tarryton said with satisfaction. 'Three real nice folk I've dealt with today at the hospital—you and young Dr Quillan and of course Dr Legrady, who's a real gentleman for a' he's foreign. Not like that cheeky laddie that was helping him last time I came to Outpatients. I'm glad *he's* gone.'

He couldn't know how the remark stabbed at her. 'Dr Dugall didn't really mean to be cross with you that day,' she murmured.

'Mebbe he didn't, mebbe he didn't. I don't think he's got the patience for doctoring. It's a good thing he's given it up.'

She glanced at him sharply. Had gossip become so strong that it had reached the patients? 'Who told you he'd given it up?'

'Why, I reckoned he had. Or was he there on holiday?'

Her grip on the old man's arm tightened convulsively.

'Where? What place? You mean you've seen Dr Dugall?'

Mr Tarryton stopped at the bus depot and turned to her with interest. 'What's wrong wi' ye? Jumped like a scalded cat when I said I'd seen him.'

'But *where*, Mr Tarryton?'

137

'In the George Inn, at Lake Wakatipu, near where I live.'

'When was this? Recently?'

'Saturday, as ever was. I was in the Public Bar, and he went by the door that leads into the residents' lounge and up t'stairs. At least I *think* it was him.'

'What was he wearing?'

'Well now, I don't rightly recall—yes, I do, though, 'twas a raincoat, a grey raincoat.'

'You didn't speak to him?'

'Not me. I wouldn't have spoken if he'd seen me, which he didn't. He walked past with his nose in the air, as usual.'

'But you think it was Dr Dugall?'

'It looked like him.' A bus drew into the depot and the old man prepared to board it. Erica helped him on.

'Guid nicht to ye, Nurse.'

'Goodnight, Mr Tarryton.'

Close to the bus depot there was a newsagent's. Erica often bought newspapers and magazines there, and was well known to its owner. She hurried in. 'Can I use your phone? I'll bring the money in later.'

'Help yourself, Nurse.'

Directory Inquiries gave her the number of the George, on Lake Wakatipu. After some difficulty she was connected. A bright genial voice said above a background of buzzing and crackling, 'George Inn, Sam Laidlaw speaking.'

'Are you the landlord?'

'Speaking. Sam Laidlaw, at your service.'

'Mr Laidlaw, have you anyone staying at the inn at present?'

'You want to book a room, do you, madam? We do take guests, yes.'

'No, I asked if you had anyone staying with you at present.'

'This line's very bad, isn't it? Would you speak up, please?'

'Is Dr Dugall there, please?'

'Who? Dr Who? This is the George Inn, not the doctor's——'

'Yes, I know it's the George Inn,' she said despairingly.

'It's the snow on the line, you know,' Mr Laidlaw said with bluff resignation. 'Always gets crook, this phone in snowy weather. Now speak up nice and loud, madam, and we'll be able to hear each other a treat.'

'Have you had anybody book a room at your inn since last week?' Erica said at her loudest pitch.

'Why, yes, miss—were you inquiring after the gentleman?'

'Yes—yes, please—could I speak to Dr Dugall?'

'Ach,' exclaimed the innkeeper in disgust, 'this isn't the doctor's house, this is the George Inn. You've got the wrong number.' And he hung up.

She reported this conversation to Sandy, who laughed a little, then looked thoughtful. 'Somebody's staying at the George, and old Mr Tarryton saw someone he thought was Ian. It sounds at least a possibility.'

'But the landlord didn't seem to recognise Ian's name at all, Sandy.'

'That figures. If he wanted to sink out of sight, he'd use an alias.'

'Yes. . . .' She made up her mind all of a sudden. 'I'm going to Wakatipu tomorrow. It's my day off. I'll take the bus Mr Tarryton boarded.'

'This isn't the weather to hang about waiting for buses. And it's a hundred and fifty miles.'

'But I feel I must go. I'm almost certain Ian is at that inn. And the most important thing in the world is to find Ian.'

Sandy looked up sharply. Then, 'Yes, of course,' he

said. 'Look here, I've a day or two's leave due to me. I'll phone in first thing tomorrow to say I'm taking the day off.'

'Will they let you have it at such short notice?'

'After I gave up my free time to them over the week-end and actually slept in the hospital in case I was needed? They'd *better*,' he said. 'Besides, I'll tell them why I want it. They'll agree.'

'You're going to say we're going in search of Ian?'

'We ought to let them know we've got a lead. But better not give his whereabouts, for ten to one Dr Matthewes will get on the phone and give Ian a lecture—and he'll resign on the spot.'

'Sandy, I'm wondering——'

'What?'

'Whether both of us ought to go?'

'Meaning Ian won't want to see me? True enough. Well, if we take my car, I can sit outside, while you go into the George to talk to Ian.'

'You're sure you want to?' she said.

'Of course I want to. I ought to try to do something to help. Just driving you up there isn't much, but it's better than nothing.'

'You ought to spend your day off getting some rest. You've been working awfully hard the last few days, Sandy. You look tired.'

'Don't you want me to come?' he said in a low voice. 'I'd be a hindrance—is that what you're trying to say?'

'Oh *no*!' She was aghast that he should think so. 'No, of course not. I'd love to have your company, Sandy, you know that.'

'You said finding Ian was the most important thing in the world,' he recalled. 'I'd like to think I'd helped you to achieve something so important, Erica.'

CHAPTER NINE

THE highway leading into the mountains from Cromwell was reasonably clear of snow. Constant traffic over the surface had melted it, while gangs of workmen sent out by winter sports authorities shovelled up the slush, and spread gravel. But the temperature was dropping rapidly and the deterioration in driving conditions was startling. The road surface was iced; over it the new snow, now falling, made a treacherous carpet. Shaking his head, Sandy drew in at a wayside garage to have the chains put on. For transport to out-of-the-way places, light aircraft or ski-planes were more popular than private cars.

The bends in the road were often masked by banks of snow which had been building up since Sunday. The front windscreen began to be patterned like lace by delicate small snowflakes. The windscreen wiper tocked back and forth, but Erica noticed that a ledge of white was forming along the outside of the glass.

'This snow is pretty thick,' she observed anxiously. 'And it seems to be falling faster.'

Sandy nodded. All his attention was for the twisting, climbing road ahead. She studied him covertly. His mouth was grim, his brow furrowed. He had said very little ever since they set out early that morning.

'Do you think we ought to go back?' she inquired.

'We're more than half-way there. Probably just as easy to go on.'

'Sandy, is anything wrong?'

'What with? The car?

'No, I meant—— Are you feeling all right? You look a bit sombre.'

'I'm all right,' he said, pushing his hair back off his forehead with an impatient gesture. 'I'm just not used to these Alpine driving conditions.'

'We'll go back if you'd rather.'

'When we're on our way to achieve the most important thing in the world? No, we'll keep going.'

There were few vehicles on the road. A big petrol tanker passed them, its wheels churning on the glassy surface. And from the opposite direction came a store delivery van driven by a white-faced man, who slowed his already slow pace to call as he went by, 'Take care up ahead!'

Erica waved and nodded. Sandy's car was in tip-top condition and Sandy's ability as a driver matched the car. She knew she was in good hands.

They went over the top of one of the many gradients and began to descend. On either hand stretched open country, tussock grassland, great untrodden expanses where the soft knolls and hollows had been smoothed to a rolling whiteness which gleamed through the strange, mottled veil of falling snow.

All of a sudden Sandy gave a sharp little exclamation. The car swerved, then went into a skid which took it careering across the road. Erica was thrown forward, but braced herself in her safety belt.

Sandy was fighting to control the car. It plunged off the road and on to the tussock, bucking like a wild horse. The tendency to spin was abruptly checked as the bonnet dived in among the grass. Nose down, back wheels shuddering a few inches off the ground, the car came to rest.

Sandy turned to Erica swiftly. His arm went round her. 'All right?'

'Yes—yes, I'm okay.

'Erica, I'm terribly sorry——'

'You couldn't help it on this terrible surface, Sandy.' She peered through the snow-spattered windows. 'Can we get back on the road?'

He opened the door his side to look at the scene. 'We ought to manage—at least I hope so.' Resuming his place, he banged the door shut and coughed. 'Air's cold out there,' he remarked with a shiver, and pulled his coat collar up.

He put the car in reverse, but the back wheels wouldn't grip. 'All right, we'll go forward, then,' he said in exasperation, but the bonnet only nosed further into the snow. He tried every manoeuvre, but the car only seemed to settle deeper at each attempt. Muttering to himself, and wiping perspiration from his forehead, he got out and walked round to the front. Almost at once he was over knee-deep in snow. He floundered a moment, then scrambled back to Erica, who was leaning out to watch him anxiously.

'We're on the edge of a hollow,' he reported, brushing the thick-falling flakes from his coat. 'There's a big snow-drift under the front wheels, so the more I try the more the front wheels sink.'

'What can we do, then, Sandy?'

He frowned. The wind whirled the snowflakes around him, and once more he drew his coat up at the collar.

'I'd no idea conditions were quite so bad,' he muttered. 'From Cromwell the roads look messy but not dangerous.'

He pressed his hand to his right side to rub against his ribs, his face screwing up in momentary pain.

'Did you hurt yourself when we skidded?' Erica asked in concern.

'May have got a bruise—no, I think I got a stitch in my side and that made me grab the wheel, and *then* we skidded. Something I've eaten, I expect. Look here, if I get to the front and push, can you guide the car out of this mess in reverse?'

'But you'll get wet through——'

'Oh, this coat's pretty thick. The heater'll soon dry me off. Honestly, Erica, there's nothing else to do. The nearest phone box is miles back. You can handle the car, can't you?'

'Yes, I think so.'

'Just slow and easy, when I give you a shout. Okay?'

It required six or seven efforts to bring the vehicle, swaying unevenly, back on all four wheels. Sandy came back and climbed in. He was soaked, and his sleeve was torn.

'Oh, Sandy, you look all in!' she cried in remorse. 'I shouldn't have let you——'

'Don't be silly, what else was there to do?' He glanced at his watch. 'Nearly one. With luck we'll be at Pelham Inlet in time for lunch. I could do with a drink. My mouth's like a lime-kiln.'

They took the road once more. Sandy's grey-blue eyes stared through the gathering curtain of snow, and his knuckles showed white as he guided the car slowly and painfully through the drifts. By and by he said, tugging at his tie to loosen the knot, 'Stuffy in here, isn't it? Mind if I open the window a crack?' When she shook her head he rolled down the glass, but a draught of icy air cut in at them like a knife blade. 'Pooh,' he said, shivering, 'we'll do without fresh air, in that case.'

Though Lake Wakatipu was only eight miles off, it took them an hour's grimly careful driving to reach it. In the shelter of the mountain slope the snow-storm was less severe and the carpet of snow on the road softer, turning to grey as the wheels passed over it. At the George Inn at Pelham Inlet a great barrel of a man was sweeping snow from the porch.

'Afternoon,' he said heartily. 'Had a right tricksy drive, eh, sir?'

'You're Mr Laidlaw, aren't you?' said Erica, recognising that beefy voice at once.

'I am. Now how did you know that? Famous, am I?'

'I spoke to you last night on the telephone. I was inquiring for Dr Dugall.'

'Ah, you're the lady, are you? Do you mean you've come out on a day like this to look for him? But I *told* you he wasn't here, now didn't I? Shame to make the journey for nothing.'

'But you have someone staying here?' she insisted.

'Not now, we haven't. No guests at all. But come in, won't you, miss? Come in, sir. Come on into the saloon. There's heating on in there.'

The saloon was plain but comfortable, with a few customers. The sudden warmth made Sandy cough, and it was left to Erica to stem the landlord's flow of talk and ask about any previous guests at the George.

'In his mid-twenties—medium height and very dark—arrived perhaps Friday night or Saturday?'

'Oh-h. . . .' His shrewd black eyes regarded Erica with anxiety. 'What's the matter? Is he in trouble? I don't want trouble, you know. . . .'

'We're friends of his,' she assured him quickly. 'There's no trouble, but we must get in touch with Dr Dugall.'

'There hasn't been a Dr Dugall staying here. But your description sounds like Mr Jones.'

'Where is Mr Jones now?'

'Left Monday.'

'You mean left the George? Or left the township?'

'Couldn't say, miss. Not a talkative lad, Mr Jones. He just paid and left.'

'Did you happen to see if he took the bus? Have you any idea at all what he intended to do?'

The landlord shook his head, and went to attend to a customer who was calling for a drink.

'Where on earth can he have gone?' Erica said miserably to Sandy. 'What are we to do now?'

Sandy made no reply. He had sat down rather wearily on a bench, and Erica, thinking of the gruelling drive he'd just accomplished, felt a pang of self-reproach.

'We'll get some lunch, shall we?' she suggested. 'And I expect you'd like a drink—what about a brandy?'

'Half a dozen cups of tea is more in my line,' he said. 'I've got a thirst like a camel.'

When the landlord came back Erica asked for something to eat and a pot of tea.

'I'll see what the missus can rustle up,' he said. 'I wasn't expecting travellers today, really. Ski folk usually come weekends. But she'll manage something.'

When Mrs Laidlaw brought the tray she gave a cry of concern for Sandy's wet clothes. 'Don't you move, sir—stay there and get dry. I'll bring this little table up to the fire'.

She was a little woman, bright and pert as a canary bird, with a quick eye that missed nothing. 'I brought stew—it's the same as we're having ourselves. Now eat it while it's hot.'

'I'm not really hungry,' Sandy said. 'I'll wait till you bring the tea.'

'Feeling a bit under the weather? Getting wet through does take it out of you.'

'No, it's this confounded indigestion——'

'I'll fetch you some mints—we have some in the bar——'

'No, don't bother, it'll go off.' When she left to fetch

the teapot he seized the opportunity of getting out of the corner in which she'd wedged him with the table. 'Whew, it's hot in here,' he complained.

He drank the tea thirstily. Mrs Laidlaw lingered.

'I hear you're asking after that quiet Mr Jones?'

Erica looked up hopefully. 'You wouldn't know where he's gone?'

'It's only a guess,' she said with satisfaction, 'but I think it's a good one. I was chatting with him on Monday—I tried to be friendly with him for he seemed so down, in himself, if you understand me. I asked him what he did for a living and he said he hadn't a job at present. "Unemployed, I am," he told me. I asked him what he'd done previously, and he said, "Wasted my time, Mrs Laidlaw, that's all I've done. What I want now is a real job of work—something I can put my back into and forget the past." '

'Plenty of work like that hereabouts,' grunted her husband, who had come to collect the cleaning gear littering the room. 'Trouble here isn't lack of work, it's lack of folk able to do it.'

'You think he's taken a job in the neighbourhood?' Erica queried, puzzled. 'Doing what?'

'Well, it may sound crook to you,' said Mrs Laidlaw, 'but he's gone to look for gold.'

'To look for——?'

'Now, Maisie, don't pull their legs. Truth is, mate,' the landlord said confidentially to Sandy, 'we get some of those old-timers in here, the kind who used to go prospecting from Arrowtown. They still sluice for gold near Skippers and all up round the snow-line. This old chap that was talking to Mr Jones, he's sure he'll strike it rich every spring. So come July and August, he starts thinking about getting his gear in good condition.'

'And he persuaded your Mr Jones to come and help

repair his cabin,' Mrs Laidlaw ended triumphantly.

'Whereabouts?' Sandy asked, pulling himself to his feet.

Erica glanced at him with concern. 'Perhaps we'd better not——'

'We can't give up now,' he said stubbornly, and turned to listen to Laidlaw's directions for finding Jerry Coult's cabin.

The fourteen miles to Height Pass were like a combat course. Erica sat with her teeth clenched together to prevent herself from crying out in alarm. It was a bad road, and with snow on top of it and snow still falling, it was a death-trap.

They would have missed the rough signpost pointing to the track if Erica hadn't been keeping a sharp lookout. Sandy backed the car and turned it into the narrow uphill drive.

'Don't know how we're ever going to get back down this again,' he muttered.

When the house came into view, Erica could have wept with relief. It was a small wooden shack with a corrugated iron roof hidden almost completely by the snow. Sandy drew up at the wicket gate that protected a yard full of snow-covered mining tools and equipment.

'You go in,' he said, leaning back exhaustedly. 'If Ian's here, he won't want to see me.'

'But you can't stay out here in the cold.'

'Why not? Besides, to tell the truth, I'm not in the mood for dealing with Ian.'

'I don't care what Ian would say. You're to come into the house, in the warm——'

'But it's warm in the car,' he pointed out. 'I don't feel like ploughing across that snow-covered yard.'

'You're sure?'

He settled back, hugging his hand to his side. 'I'm beginning to wish I'd taken Mrs Laidlaw up on the offer of the soda-mint,' he said wryly. 'I think I'll have a snooze.' He leaned back and closed his eyes. Then he opened them again. 'Good luck.'

Seeing that he really meant it, Erica closed the car door. Perhaps a rest would do him good.

She forced open the gate against the snow. The short walk to the front door left her with wet shoes and stockings. The snow blew against her tweed coat, catching in the coloured flecks of wool. It blew into her eyes, into her nostrils, down inside her coat collar.

Reaching the little porch was like entering a haven. She knocked on the door.

A tall, stooped old man in tweed trousers, grey sweater, and several waistcoats opened the door. 'Thought I heard summat. Lost your way?'

'No, I'm looking for Jerry Coult.'

'That's me.' He was surprised.

'You're Mr Coult?'

'Aye.'

'Have you a Mr Jones working for you?'

'Ah.' He drew bushy grey eyebrows together. 'I knew he spelt trouble. Wouldn't have hired him, only I wanted that shed finished. So you're after Jones, are you?'

'I'd like to speak to him, if I may.'

'Better come in, or you'll have the place full of snow. Wipe your feet.'

Obediently Erica did so. He led the way into a small roughly-furnished room, but made no offer of a chair.

'Now,' he said sternly, 'why do you want him? What's he done?'

'Nothing,' she replied. 'I just want to talk to him.'

'You his wife? Has he run off and left you?'

'I'm no relation, Mr Coult. Just a friend.'

'Right fond friend, you must be, to come all this way in this weather. I don't know whether I should let you bother him. It's his own business if he wants to find some peace and quiet. Besides, he's busy.'

'He can't be building a shed in this weather,' she protested.

'No, more's the pity, for I wanted it done afore the snow started again so I could get my gear under cover. But he's busy, for all that. He's doing my accounts for me.'

'I really would like to see him,' pleaded Erica. 'It's very important.'

'But ten to one if I let you see him, you'll persuade him to leave here. And I've only just hired him. Hard to get help in these parts. Fellers don't like the tough life.'

She said nothing to this. She waited, looking earnestly at the old man. Finally she shrugged and gave in. He went through a door in the back of the room and shouted.

'Jones! Jones, here a minute!'

'Did you call, Mr Coult?'

The voice was unmistakably Ian's. At least the first phase of the mission was accomplished.

But now came the more difficult part. She had to persuade him to come back to Reidmouth.

He came in at the door of the living-room. He was wearing borrowed clothes—corduroy slacks and a thick brown pullover. At the sight of Erica his face lit up in disbelieving welcome. Then recollection swept over it, like a cloud passing over the sun.

'What are you doing here?' he asked in an icy tone. 'Did Legrady give you permission?'

'Ian, we've all been worried to death over you! Why didn't you let us know where you'd gone?'

'It wasn't anyone's business.'

'Not even your mother's? Haven't you given her a thought?'

'Have you been badgering her?' he flashed. 'Why did you have to drag her in?'

'Naturally the Superintendent thought you'd gone home. He tried to get in touch with you there. As it happened, your mother wasn't at home to answer the telephone. I went there looking for you and broke the news to her.'

'And gave her a thoroughgoing fright, I've no doubt. Why can't you keep out of my affairs?'

'Ah, that's a thing no woman can do,' put in Jerry Coult. 'They love to meddle, all of them!'

Erica glanced aside at the old man. 'Could I speak to you alone, Ian?'

'We've nothing to say to each other.'

'Please, Ian. I've come a long way——'

'That's your concern,' Coult said. 'Besides, I'm paying Jones to work for me, not chat to you.'

'I'll pay you anything you think you're losing by letting us talk a few minutes,' she retorted.

'Hoity-toity! Got a temper, eh? You watch out for her, my lad!' He went to the door, and paused. 'Ten minutes I'll give you. After that, there's work to be done, and don't you forget it's what I took you on for. I ain't got money to waste.'

He stamped out, obviously indignant at being shown he was in the way. Erica directed her level gaze at Ian.

'Are you out of your mind, taking a job with a mean old curmudgeon like that?'

'What I do is my own affair entirely——'

'No, it isn't—and don't let's waste time pretending it is. There's your mother to consider——'

'It's because of my mother I'm in this mess,' he said with a deep, perplexed bitterness. 'Trying to live up to what she expected, trying to be what I'm not! Well, that's all over now. I'm finished with pretence. It's time the world knew that the only resemblance between my father and me is the name.'

'You're really determined to give up your career?'

'Yes, quite determined.'

'Then at least come back to Reidmouth and say so to the Medical Superintendent! To run away without a word is childish.'

He hesitated. 'I'll—I'll write to him.'

'Ashamed to face him?'

'Not a bit.' He was vehement. 'There's nothing to be ashamed of in changing your mind.'

'Even when you're throwing away six years of training, six years of study?'

'It's better to realise it's a mistake and get out before it's too late. Don't you understand, Erica? People's lives would have depended on me—on *me*—and I haven't any confidence, any ability.'

'But that's not true. Believe me, Ian, it's not true. Sandy thinks——'

'Sandy thinks! Sandy thinks! There's an example of what I mean. Six years of training, as you say—but all the while I need someone else to bolster my morale. When I get in a flap at the hospital, you or Sandy have to rescue me. What's going to happen when neither of you is at hand? What do I do then? Oh, don't you see, it's hopeless.'

'At least come back and talk it over with Dr Matthewes. You can't make a decision like this all in a moment, and especially at a time when you're feeling hurt and unhappy.' She touched his arm, a gesture of timid appeal. 'Ian, I know I've bungled my attempts to help you, but this time I feel I'm giving you good advice. Come back to Reidmouth. If you don't, I'll always feel it's my fault.'

'Nothing's your fault, Erica. You've done your best. I

don't bear you any ill-will. I've just come to the realisation that I'm a misfit.'

'But you're not. Sandy believes you have the capacity to be good at your job if only you'll stop worrying about it. He brought me here today. He's outside in the car. Speak to him—let him tell you what he thinks of your fitness for the work.'

'I don't want to see him,' he burst out. 'I refuse to see him.'

'But after we've made this long journey——? We've had a terrible time getting here. We nearly overturned once. Sandy's about all in. If we're willing to make such an effort——'

'I'm sorry. I appreciate that you're really trying to help. But I don't want any more discussion. My decision's made.'

'You'll regret it all your life.'

'I don't think so. There must be other things I could do. If the worst comes to the worst I can always go to an employment bureau and ask for a job. I might do quite well in some line of business where I'm not expected to live up to my father.'

'Ian, promise me at least to get in touch with your mother.'

'No! I don't want her to know where I am.'

'But she's beside herself with worry——'

'No, I tell you! She'll only try to persuade me back to the life I dread——'

'She won't do that, Ian. She says you can do whatever you like. She only wants you to be happy. Ian, please— write to her.'

'Well, all right,' he said unwillingly. 'I will by and by. You can tell her I'm all right and I'm sorry if she's been worried.'

She turned to the door. 'Won't you please come with us,

Ian? You can't really hope to achieve anything here. The gold in these mountains was worked out fifty years ago. Mr Coult is living in the past. Come back with us to the present.'

'No, I'm staying here.'

'You're making a dreadful mistake.'

'I don't think so. Goodbye, Erica.'

As soon as her hand touched the door-knob the door swung open. Coult had been standing behind it all the time, probably eavesdropping.

'Had a nice chat?' he said in sardonic inquiry.

'Miss Ryall is just leaving,' said Ian.

'Good day to ye,' the old man said. 'And don't waste any time getting started, or you'll find yourself in difficulties. As for you, lad—what about those supplies of mine you were checking?'

He took Ian by the elbow and steered him back along the passage. Erica was left to see herself out.

The wind had risen considerably. She had to fight her way across the yard. As she reached the gate, above the whine of the wind, she heard a recurrent sound—a short dry cough, repeated several times. She thought the old man had come to the house door, and looked back, but the door was closed.

Then she understood two things—the nature of the cough and the fact that it was coming from the car.

The gate stood open, blocked this way by the snow. She hurried through, and her view of the car became clearer. Sandy had rolled down the windows for air.

Half-melted snowflakes had caught in his hair, drifted in from the open windows. He was bent over the steering wheel, his head pillowed on one arm.

She wrenched open the car door. 'Sandy!' At the sound of her voice he pulled himself upright with a tremendous effort. She saw that his other hand was pressed hard against his side. His face was highly flushed, his eyes when

154

he saw her struggled to focus. She saw him drag himself back from the rim of unconsciousness.

'Erica,' he said in recognition.

'Sandy, you're burning with fever!' She touched his cheek, and then slipped her arm about him as a support.

'About a hundred and three, at a guess,' he gasped, with a desperate attempt at a smile. He was overtaken by the cough as he spoke.

'Don't try to talk. Just answer yes or no. Your chest hurts?'

'Classic symptoms of pneumonia. Just recognized them. Fine doctor, eh? Thought—indigestion. Pneumococcus from hospital patients.'

'But it's come on so suddenly and severely, Sandy!'

'Felt queer yesterday. Sloshing about today—snow. Tired. Worried.' He coughed. 'Might not have developed till—tomorrow—in other—circumstances.'

Every breath he took cost him a gasp of pain. He began to shiver, and she pulled his coat around him, only to discover it was sodden. She checked a sob of dismay which rose in her throat.

Sandy seemed to remember something. 'Ian . . .' he said hazily.

'He's not coming.'

'Pity . . . I need his help . . . more than he ever . . . needed mine.'

He struggled against the wave of darkness, but his strength was ebbing. His eyes slid shut. His weight became heavy on her arm.

She fought down a rising tide of panic. They were miles away from anywhere in the middle of the worst weather of the winter.

And the unconscious man she held in her arms was dangerously ill.

CHAPTER TEN

CAREFULLY Erica settled Sandy into the corner of the car. As carefully, she worked her arm free. Then hurrying back up the path, she knocked on the door. There was no reply, and she knocked again, louder and with urgency.

A voice spoke from behind the door. Mr Coult must have been standing behind it, waiting to hear the car drive off.

'Go away,' he said. 'You've wasted enough of our time.'

'Open the door. I've got to speak to Ian!'

'You already have.'

'But this is different—I need his help! Open the door, Mr Coult!'

She heard him shuffle away, and in angry desperation she hammered on the door. When she stopped, it was to hear Mr Coult speaking to Ian.

'—Only a trick to make you go with her.'

'Erica's not like that. Get out of my way!'

She heard what sounded almost like a scuffle. Then Ian swung the door open. She grasped his arm.

'It's Sandy—he's in a state of collapse——'

His eyes widening in alarm, he hurried past her. Snow clothed him in white in a moment. He paused to brush off the flakes before leaning into the car to look at Sandy.

'How long's he been like this?'

'Since I came into the house. But he complained of a stitch in his side earlier—before lunch—that was what caused us to skid. That made us hit a snowdrift, and he had to heave us out. He got soaked. Since then he's been shivery and thirsty. Oh, I should have noticed! But my mind was taken up with getting to you and making you come back.'

'Of course there was a lot of pneumonia at Reidmouth . . .' He pursed his lips. 'We'd better get him into the house and phone for an airlift.'

The old man, overcome by curiosity, had followed them gingerly down the path. Ian swung round on him and said with authority, 'Give me a hand, and be careful how you go.'

Unquestioningly Coult obeyed. Between them they carried him into the room where Erica had already been, and laid him on an old-fashioned leather sofa.

'Have you some blankets?' Erica asked.

'Blankets?' Coult repeated. 'To wrap round a sick man? Do you want me to catch whatever it is he's got?'

Ian, who was about to go to the phone, looked back. 'We need blankets and a change of clothes for him, and a warm drink, and some heating for this room.'

'Oh, now, look here——'

'He's seriously ill. He'll get worse rapidly unless he has at least the minimum of comfort. Can you find it in your conscience to refuse him that?'

Without bothering to say more he strode away. Erica heard him pick up a telephone in the other room and ask the exchange for the ambulance service. Then her attention was taken up with doing what she could for Sandy, helped unwillingly but competently by Coult.

He had brought an old-fashioned kerosene heater into the room when Ian came back. Ian eyed it, surveyed the clutter of maps and boots and fishing rods, and frowned.

'It's going to be a long wait for the ambulance. Can't we do better than this for him?'

'What's wrong with this?' Coult demanded indignantly. 'My best room, this is.'

'Yes, but the sofa looks as hard as a board. And I suppose you can't light the fire without unloading all that gear you've stored in the fireplace.'

'Why should I light a fire? Hasn't been a fire in this grate for over thirty years. See here,' said Mr Coult, 'I don't mind offering a bit of hospitality, but lighting fires is going too far. My woodpile's got to last me all winter.'

'Mr Coult, I want my patient in a room where I can have plenty of fresh air with adequate warmth——'

'Your patient!' jeered the old man. 'Stop playing at doctors, lad.'

'I'm not playing. I am a doctor.'

'Now don't tell lies——'

'Quite . . . true . . .' said Sandy's voice. 'A good doctor too. . . .'

Erica bent over him. His eyes were open and full of awareness. His glance flickered round the room.

'Not hospital . . .?'

'We're waiting for an airlift, Sandy.'

'Aye, and a right long wait you'll have,' Coult said in disgust. 'Nothing's going to fly in this weather. In any case, they never come up this valley—too dicey. You might have got away in your car if you'd started half an hour ago, but it's been snowing a blizzard since then and you'd likely get stuck at the hollow a mile down the slope.'

'We couldn't risk it with Sandy in this state,' Ian said. 'How long do you think the snow is likely to go on?'

'That's set in for the night, that has. It'll leave snowdrifts thick enough to block us up here two days, maybe three.'

'*Three days?*' cried Erica.

'Tcha, that ain't long. Two winters out of three, Heights Pass is cut off for half a week at a time—sometimes longer. The winter of 1940, I recall, it took 'em fifteen days before they dug the road clear. Makes no difference to me. Nobody's going to come nigh the place, nor nobody leave it. Not you, nor him——' nodding at Sandy.

Ian was frowning. 'What about the nearest doctor?'

'Thought you said you were one?'

'But I haven't any medicines. I need sulpha drugs——' He broke off to lean over Sandy and speak gently. 'I say, old man, got anything useful in your car?'

'First aid kit ... One or two instruments ... All my stuff—at hospital.'

Ian nodded. 'And of course when I walked out I left my bag and everything else. Blithering idiot that I was!' He addressed Coult. 'What about the local doctor, then?'

'His number's Heights 23. But he lives a goodish piece away—near the Becky Bridge. I'll take a wager *he* won't get here, either.'

Ian went back to the telephone. Sandy whispered, 'Erica, don't forget ... ring the hospital ... and explain.'

'I'll do it at once. Don't worry about it, Sandy dear— and don't talk any more.'

The old prospector led the way to the room he used as store-room and office, where the telephone stood. Ian was just replacing the receiver.

'Dr Princeton's wife says he's stranded at a house on Blundel Side.'

'Aye, I reckon,' Coult said with enjoyment. 'Another brat, I expect. And *we'll* be in touch with the world again before the houses on Blundel Side.'

'So we can't expect help from that quarter.'

'No, you can't. You're in a rare fix, aren't you?'

Erica found his malicious amusement hard to bear. 'May I use your telephone?' she asked coldly.

'Oh, go ahead! You'll cost me a fortune in telephone charges and extra heating, between you!'

'Look here, Mr Coult, it's obvious we're stuck here overnight at least, with a very sick man. If I promise to pay you for anything we use, will you drop this penny-pinching attitude?'

'You'll pay, will you? Can I have that in writing?'

'If you think it's necessary.' Ian's voice was hard. 'Now I want a room with heating and a proper bed, and I'd like to inspect your medicine cabinet to see if you've got anything helpful. What else, Erica?'

'Plenty of blankets, and pillows, and towels, and a sponge. And barley water or lemonade, or anything like that. What about brandy or whisky, Ian?'

'I'll have a look. Come on, Coult, let's get a room ready while Erica phones.'

She got through to the hospital after some delay and two wrong connections. It was growing dark outside; a glance at her watch showed her it was nearly four o'clock. Matron might be at a meeting at such an hour. She was relieved to hear the crisp cool voice at last.

'Matron? This is Staff Nurse Ryall speaking.'

'Who? Staff Nurse Ryall? It doesn't sound like you a bit.'

'I'm speaking from Heights Pass, in the mountains north of Lake Wakatipu, Matron. We——'

'From where? What on earth are you doing there?'

'Dr Legrady and I came here to look for Dr Dugall. We both had the day off, you see——'

'But what on earth made you think you'd find Dr Dugall *there*?'

'One of our out-patients thought he'd seen him in the

160

district. It turns out he was right too.'

'You mean you've found Dr Dugall?'

'Yes, Matron.'

'Oh, well *done*, Staff Nurse! Now you must bring him back to the hospital at once, and the whole matter——'

'I can't do that, Matron. You see, Dr Legrady's been taken ill——' She broke off. She found she was no longer in control of her voice.

'Hello? Hello? Dear me, not *another* breakdown? Hello, Nurse! Nurse Ryall! Are you still there?'

'Yes, Matron, I'm still here. I was trying to say that Dr Legrady had been taken very ill with pneumonia——'

'Good heavens! Have you sent for the flying ambulance? We'll get a bed ready for him at once!'

'Dr Dugall sent for the ambulance, but they say there will be a delay. Mr Coult, who owns the place, says he doesn't think the ambulance will get through before to-morrow at the earliest.'

'You mean you're cut off?'

'I'm afraid so. The snow is very bad up here, you see.'

'But, my dear girl, it can't be as bad as that?' Matron caught herself up. 'Well, of course, I know it can. In previous winters I've known it take several days. . . . How is Dr Legrady?'

'Very feverish, and in pain.'

'From the inflammation of the pleura—yes. What exactly are you able able to do for him?'

'We're trying to make him as comfortable as possible. The house-owner is not very co-operative. Dr Dugall is— Dr Dugall has taken charge.'

'Has he indeed? Very well, Staff Nurse. I'll inform Dr Galland immediately and get him to ring Dr Dugall with advice and instructions. I will also see that every effort is made to reach you. How are your yourself, Staff Nurse?'

'Quite well, Matron. Only very worried.'

'You do realise that you shouldn't have undertaken a journey that was likely to prevent you from reporting for duty at the proper time?'

'Yes, Matron. I'm sorry.'

'Do your best to give Dr Dugall every assistance. I'll speak to you again when Dr Galland rings.'

Erica hurried to the living-room, where the voices of the men could be heard. She reported the conversation to Ian, who was setting a match to the fire he had laid in the grate. Coult was tugging at a window which looked as if it hadn't been open for the last ten years. He broke off to tell Erica that sheets were airing in front of the kitchen stove, and that he and Ian would bring a bed from one of the other rooms. The old man looked annoyed when Ian succeeded in opening the window.

'The damp'll get in,' he said. 'And I don't like the way that chap keeps coughing. Is it anything infectious, what he's got?'

'He's got lobar pneumonia,' said Ian.

'Pneumonia, has he?' Coult looked impressed. 'My old mother, God rest her soul, was carried off by the pneumonia just before the war. A real death-dealer it was, before they had these new wonder drugs.' All at once the gravity of the situation seemed to strike him with its full force. A gleam of horrified alarm came into his pebble-like old eyes 'You haven't got these new drugs either, though, have you?'

'No, Mr Coult, we haven't.'

'Lordamercy, he stands a slim chance, then, doesn't he?'

Ian made a stifled sound. She turned her head to look at him.

'It's my fault,' he said. 'If it hadn't been for me you

162

two wouldn't be out in this icy wilderness.'

'But you couldn't possibly foresee——'

'No, I couldn't foresee this, but if I'd stopped brooding about myself and thought what a trouble I was being to everyone else——! If anything happens to Sandy, it'll be my fault.'

'Don't think of it like that. Besides, nothing is going to happen to him. You and I will see him through until help comes.'

He drew a deep breath. Then he held out his hand.

'You and I together.'

The expected call from Dr Galland never came through. About seven o'clock they tried to ring the hospital, but couldn't even get the exchange.

'The wire's down,' said Coult with a shrug.

By ten o'clock that evening, despite all they could do, Sandy's temperature was still climbing. He was tossing and muttering, a broken string of unconnected phrases interspersed with coughing.

'He'll come back, Dr Matthewes ... Only nerves ... can't be blamed for nerves ... Another chance, Dr Matthewes, give him another chance ...'

Ian and Erica had cradled the bedclothes on a frame Ian had knocked up from scraps of wood. Across the bed his glance met hers. He looked ashamed.

'And this is the man I'd decided was my enemy,' he said.

'Perhaps for a while he felt the same about you,' she admitted. 'But his views altered. He got worried about you, Ian—he said you were heading for disaster.'

'He was right, wasn't he? I could scarcely have made a bigger hash of things. If only I could do something about it—if I could have another chance!'

'There's no reason why not.'

'After this?' Ian's hand flung out, indicating their present plight.

Sandy's coughing prevented Ian from saying more of what was in his mind. After the bout had passed, Sandy said quite clearly, 'Erica.'

'Yes, Sandy. I'm here.'

'If only she cared for me . . . No hope now . . . Most important thing in the world is Ian . . . Erica and Ian . . . We'll find him, because he's the most important . . . to Erica. . . .'

'Does he really believe that?' Ian said incredulously.

Erica dared not look up. 'I think he does.'

'And is it true?'

'It's what I told him last night—that finding you was the most important thing in the world. I was so worried about you, Ian. I had to find you and bring you to your senses.'

Ian went to the fire and stared into it. 'I won't ask you what more it might mean. It's not the time for personal matters. But whatever your answer turns out to be, one thing's certain. I've had friends that I didn't know how to value. In future I'm going to behave more like a sensible human being and less like an armadillo!'

Sandy's restlessness increased. His delirium grew alarming. He was talking now in a mutter of Hungarian, a language Erica had scarcely ever heard him use.

'Can't you do anything for him, Ian?' she cried. 'The pain in his chest is exhausting him and the fever's burning him up. Help him, Ian, help him!'

Ian clasped and unclasped his hands in desperation.

'The only medicines in the house are that disgusting collection in the box in the kitchen. He needs medinal or luminal—something like that. We just haven't got them.'

'Isn't there anything in the box that would do? Just to ease the pain a little, and let him get some rest?'

'Most of the bottles have got no labels, and though there are one or two packets in chemist's white paper, they're mouldering away in pieces.' His eyes darted to the tossing figure on the bed. 'But we've got to do something. I'll go and have another look.'

She heard him hurry to the store-room. He was gone some time, and she was too busy trying to look after Sandy to wonder what he was doing.

About half an hour later he came back into the room. He sat down rather heavily on the wooden chair near the window, and said to Erica, 'There was some stuff in a carved Maori box—a mixture of herbs and what looked like mineral salts. Jerry Coult says it's an old Maori pain-killer he was given years ago by a pal who used to go prospecting with him.'

'Yes?' Erica said eagerly. She knew that many old traditional remedies had useful properties, and placed as they were now they had only traditional methods to call on.

'I brewed some of this stuff in a drop of boiling water and took it, Erica—about half an hour ago.'

'Ian, you didn't!' She was startled. Though of course, when she stopped to think, there was no other way of testing the drug except by trying it on someone. 'You should have let me——'

'No fear. Anyhow, I think we'll find it helpful. It's made me feel jolly lethargic, and sleepy, so if we make an infusion and give it to Sandy, it may help to dull that pain he's undergoing. What I want to know is—should we administer it?'

Erica clasped her hands in an agony of uncertainty. Had they the right to take such a risk? But if they did not, Sandy's temperature might never stop climbing; the result would be total exhaustion of the kind that, in Victorian times, had meant death to pneumonia cases.

But then Ian stood up. 'I'm the one who must decide,' he said. 'After all, I'm supposed to be the one who prescribes for my patient. And I say we *must* try this old remedy, Erica. If we don't, I doubt if Sandy will last through the night.'

Erica went to him and kissed him gently on the cheek. 'I know he couldn't be in better hands,' she said.

Half an hour later they stood together watching as their patient sank into a much-needed sleep. 'That's something, at least,' muttered Ian. 'If we can ease his chest pain and lower his temperature so that he doesn't get light-headed and toss about . . . By heaven, it must have been a life and death fight for every patient in the days before the sulpha drugs!'

'I think it was,' Erica agreed, lowering the light in the pressure lamp for fear it should disturb Sandy. 'Sister Tutor used to tell us we didn't know what real nursing was these days, because of all the new discoveries.'

'Maybe I didn't know what "real doctoring" was,' Ian murmured. 'I'm beginning to understand it now. I feel I can't bear to go out of the room in case there's some change. . . .'

'All the same, we must get some rest. We've got the rest of the night before us—and for all we know the ambulance may not get through until late tomorrow—or even not till next day, if this gale keeps blowing.'

'Oh, let's hope it's soon. That packet of powder won't last for ever, and for all I know it's not really suitable—I mean, it's got all sorts of impurities in it from lying in that mouldy old box. Oh, Erica, I'd give my soul for a supply of sulphathiazole!'

'I know, I know—but until it comes we must just do

166

everything we can think of to help him. I'm going to find us some food, and after that we ought to think about sleep.'

'We'll take it in turns. I'll take the first shift.'

Erica lay down in the cold little room assigned to her by their host, but she didn't sleep. She watched the snow fall in hurried, unrelenting deluge. Each snowflake added a tiny scrap of weight in the scale against Sandy. As the snowdrifts thickened, the chances of help receded.

They had nothing with which to fight except a few primitive medicines, their united skill as nurse and doctor, and their determination not to give in. Against them were ranged the bitter weather, the lack of modern drugs, and a killer infection which in days gone by had claimed one in four of those who contracted it.

'One in four. One in four.' It tolled like the ringing of a death knell in her ears.

By and by she looked at her watch and realised that Ian should have come to rouse her by now. She got out of bed and tiptoed along the passage to the sickroom.

Ian was sitting on a chair by the bed. His hand lay on the covers, ready at the least movement to come to his patient's help.

But he had fallen asleep. His head drooped forward on his chest. He looked very young, very immature and very defenceless.

She took one of the spare pillows and, easing him gently back against it, let him settle to a more comfortable position for sleep. Then she went to the window to watch the snow, glancing back every now and again to make sure that all was still well.

She would fight, she would work, she would do all she could. But unless help came, the chances were still: 'One in four. One in four.'

CHAPTER ELEVEN

Two days later, in the morning, a strange sound broke the stillness of the snow-clad world. A throbbing, droning sound.

'A plane!' grunted Coult. 'Fancy them sending a plane to Heights Pass! Never happened before.'

The snow had ceased to fall on the previous day about noon. The wind seemed milder although it had by no means died completely. But perhaps lower in the valley the conditions had improved enough for a ski-plane to get through.

It churred up the pass towards them. Erica was at the downstairs window, watching. She gave an exclamation of incredulity when she realised what she saw.

The plane had landed, and from it had stepped no one else but the hospital's dignified Medical Consultant, Dr Aloysius Galland. He was muffled to the eyes in scarves and topcoats, and he looked very apprehensive.

The pilot was identified by Jerry Coult as 'that lazy Bob Flackland'. Bob handed Dr Galland down from the plane, grinning.

Dr Galland clumped in as Erica held the house door open for him. To his chest the consultant was clutching a box.

'Well,' he said without preamble, 'how is he?'

'Holding his own, sir. Dr Dugall has done wonders for him, considering the difficulties.'

'Glad to hear it. If he'd let him die I'd have taken him up in that plane and thrown him out at six thousand feet.

You look as if you haven't had much sleep recently, young woman. Well, come on, show me to my patient.'

Erica turned to lead the way. Ian had come half-way from the store-room to see the reason for all the noise, and at sight of his chief stood looking both scared and relieved.

'Good—good morning, sir,' he stammered.

'Humph,' said Galland, 'I'll speak to you later. Where is Legrady?'

'In here, sir.'

The consultant paused outside the door to divest himself of several layers of clothing. Then, with an unexpectedly gentle tread, he went into the room and up to the bed.

'Well, my dear fellow? How are you?'

'Still alive,' whispered Sandy. 'Thanks to Dr Dugall and Staff Nurse Ryall.'

'Only just, though,' said Dr Galland. 'I bet you're glad to see this.' He tapped the box. 'Sulphathiazole.'

'What,' said Sandy with the ghost of a smile, 'no grapes?'

'Keep quiet. Nurse, I want to examine my patient.'

Erica stepped forward in automatic obedience. While Dr Galland conducted his examination he talked. 'Humph. Base of right lung as dull as a block of wood. Right, we'll start treatment right away. Then it's you for a nice cosy bed in the hospital. How does that sound?'

'Sounds fine,' Sandy agreed in a husky voice.

'Right. Now then, Dugall, you go out to that infernal contraption. There's a box of grub—fruit juice, meat extract, and so on. There's a portable oxygen set—I thought we might need it and you'd better bring it in. There's a drug case—morphia and penicillin. I brought everything I could think of because, not being able to get in touch by phone, I didn't know what to expect.' He paused and added guardedly, 'I must say you don't seem to have done too badly, considering the conditions. Your patient is extremely weak, but you seem to have kept him from getting lightheaded. Nevertheless, if he'd had to go through the old-style "crisis", I wouldn't have given much for his chances. Luckily we'll be able to prevent that now.'

'I'm extremely glad you came, sir. We hadn't much in the way of a drug supply.'

'I imagine not. You've done well, Dugall—but that doesn't excuse your conduct.'

'No, sir.'

'Well, go and get those things in, then.'

'Yes, sir.'

It was amazing how the arrival of Dr Galland and his modern equipment removed the haunting nightmare element from the house. The improvement in Sandy's condition was dramatic; his temperature began to drop at once, his pulse and respiration returned almost to normal. He went quietly to sleep and in that sleep began to regain the strength that had been consumed by fighting the fever of pneumonia.

Ian wasn't much in evidence. After Dr Galland arrived to take charge of the treatment he withdrew quietly into the background. Erica, on the other hand, found her work increased. Whereas Ian had shared every task with her, the consultant naturally expected the nursing to be her concern solely.

But she was too happy to think of complaining. Sandy was going to be all right.

The plane took off late that day, and they returned in it to Cromwell. They had a typical farewell from Mr Coult.

'What about that shed I hired you to build?' he said angrily to Ian.

'I'm afraid you'll have to build it on your own.'

'But I thought you didn't want to go back to Reidmouth?'

'I thought so too. But I was wrong.'

'Ah well, then, here's your bill.' He presented a paper.

Ian unfolded it, glanced at it, and gasped. 'But this is more like four days at the Ritz than four days in a cold, draughty old shack!'

'Ah! Trying to get out of paying, is that it? I knew I should have made you put it in writing!'

'I'll send you the money,' Ian said. 'But if ever you come into the hospital as a patient, I hope I handle your case.'

'That isn't very likely,' the old man said in triumph. 'For one thing I don't hold with hospitals, for another I hear you're going to get the sack.'

This was the general opinion in the hospital, so Erica found. Every friend or acquaintance who came to her room and, under pretext of inquiring after her health, prevented her from catching up with her lost sleep, voiced the same opinion: 'Ian Dugall's *for* it.'

'What do you think will happen?' she asked Sandy when she went to visit him on Sunday.

'It sounds as if he's going to be hung, drawn and quartered. I hear Matthewes is furious with him.'

'I suppose he has reason to be.'

'Well, first of all Ian went missing, and then he caused you to go missing and me to go missing, and finally Galland took off for the back of beyond—though Galland announced his plans beforehand. With the winter ailments flowing in and the usual mob of bad weather accidents, the hospital has been hard pressed. You can understand the Superintendent's viewpoint.'

'Is there anything anybody could do?'

'I think I could do a lot,' Sandy muttered. 'I know the

case—I know what caused all the trouble and I could put it so as to sound less irresponsible on Ian's part. But I'm still under Galland's orders. That's the worst of being a patient in the hospital you work for—you have to do as you're told. If we can manage to put off the meeting of the Appointments Sub-Committee until I'm up and about, I think I could be a help.'

'Who else is on the Sub-Committee?'

'Well, Galland, as Senior Medical Consultant. And Sir Vian Partick, our Chairman. And Matthewes makes the third. If I know Matthewes he'll be on the phone first thing tomorrow morning, getting it fixed up. He hates delay.'

'But if the others couldn't fit it in very soon?'

'He'd have to put off the meeting until it suited them all.'

'I see.' She got up and stood indecisive for a moment. 'I think I'll go and see a few people,' she said.

'Oh.' He was disappointed. 'This has been a short visit. Are you going to meet Ian?'

'No, Ian is with his mother. She flew in the day before yesterday. He's been suspended, of course, so he's got plenty of time to go around with her and talk to her and so forth. I think it's a good thing. It's time those two came to an understanding about what's so important about a career in medicine!'

Sandy wriggled about on his pillows as a man will do when he feels fit and well and restless and yet must stay in bed. 'Come and see me again tomorrow,' he begged. 'It's awfully boring being a patient.'

'I'll be on duty tomorrow.'

'Well, pop in as you pass. Won't you, Erica?' he added pleadingly.

She smiled. 'All right.'

When she did so, she had news for him. 'I've made sure

the Appointments Sub-Committee won't meet until a week next Wednesday.'

'You've made sure?' Sandy sat up so suddenly that his book slid off his lap and landed on the floor. Erica picked it up and handed it back. He stared at her. 'How did you manage that?'

'Well, first of all I went to see Dr Galland.'

'You did *what*?'

'I went to see him. At his home.'

'When?'

'Yesterday. Have you ever been there, Sandy? It's a nice house, but oh, that horrible pseudo-Elizabethan furniture!'

'Never mind his furniture, what did he say?'

'I explained that you thought you could help Ian's case if you were allowed to speak at the inquiry. But of course you were being kept in bed——'

'Lot of silly nonsense,' grumbled Sandy. 'I feel as fit as a fiddle.'

'You know you wouldn't if you got up,' she scolded. 'But you'll be all right by Wednesday week.'

'But why Wednesday week?'

'It was the first day that came into my mind. Dr Galland gave me an awfully old-fashioned look and said "Very well, Staff Nurse, which day shall I note in my diary as suitable for this meeting?" And I just said "Wednesday week." '

'Didn't he bite your head off?' Sandy asked in amazement.

'No. Actually he was rather nice.' She coloured a little as she recalled the kind things that the consultant had actually said about her work at the shack on Heights Pass. Still, that wasn't the sort of thing one repeated. It would sound like self-glorification.

'You're amazing, Erica. You really are. Well, and so Galland isn't going to be free for this meeting until Wednesday week, which means I'll get a chance to be there. Good-o!'

'I'm going to be there too,' Erica said, looking down nervously at her hands.

'You? Why?'

'It's Matron's idea. She's rather keen to do all she can on Ian's behalf because she once nursed at St Gregory's under Ian's father. Between you, me and the gatepost, I think Matron had a very soft spot for Ian Dugall Senior. At any rate, she thinks I might be able to add something useful, and she's sent my name in.'

'Poor old Erica! Never mind, it won't be so bad. Sir Vian's a nice old man, and from what you say you've got Galland eating out of your hand. So all we do is concentrate our fire on Dr Matthewes. He's the one who's out for Ian's blood.'

'What actually could they do to him, Sandy?'

He thought carefully before he answered. 'At the best, they could tick him off and let it go at that. At the worst, they could actually dismiss him.'

'Oh, they wouldn't do that? Oh no, Sandy, it would be too cruel. Especially now, when he's discovered that he desperately wants to be a doctor after all.'

'What is more likely to happen,' said Sandy, 'is that they'll put down a very nasty black mark against his name. That would follow him wherever he went for years to come—"irresponsible" or "not conscientious". It would take him a while to build up his reputation again. He could do it, but it would take time. It would be better if it could be prevented.'

'Then we must do our very best for him on Wednesday week,' she replied emphatically.

CHAPTER TWELVE

On Wednesday week, at three-thirty in the afternoon, Sandy and Erica sat outside the door of the committee room waiting to be called. Ian was inside, explaining his conduct.

'Do you think we'll be called in singly, or together?' Erica asked nervously.

'Which would you prefer?'

'Oh, together,' she said with fervour. 'I'm no good at speaking up before important people.'

'Then together it shall be,' he said.

She studied him. He still hadn't regained the weight he'd lost during his illness, though he looked well. Yet there was a quietness about him; not exactly as if he were tired, but as if life didn't seem quite so enjoyable as it used to.

'You're feeling all right these days?' she asked.

'Right as rain. I'm going home for a week's holiday, to benefit from some of my mama's home-cooking, and then after that it's back to work. Thank heaven,' he added. 'I hate being at a loose end. Gives you too much time to think.'

'Why? What do you think about?' she asked.

'The future, mainly. I'll soon be leaving Reidmouth, Erica. My four years as Registrar will be up in November.'

'Ian's contract is up at the end of October.' She looked at Sandy in some dismay. 'Reidmouth's going to get awfully empty all of a sudden.'

'I shall be sorry to go,' he answered.

'You've been applying for consultant vacancies, haven't you, Sandy? Any luck?'

'One or two interviews coming up. I don't know how they'll go.'

'Oh, but that's good! To have been short-listed for interview is half the battle.'

He shrugged. At that moment the door opened and Ian came out, looking white. At their look of anxious inquiry he made a grimace.

'The general opinion seems to be that I'm a thoughtless idiot and behaved like one. They're quite right, of course.'

The committee room door opened. The Superintendent's secretary put her head out. 'Staff Nurse Ryall, please.'

Erica jumped to her feet, looking imploringly at Sandy. He came with her to the door.

'Miss O'Donovan, would you ask the committee if they would take me first?'

'Oh, I don't think they——Sir Vian said——'

Dr Galland, from his vantage point at the end of the boardroom table, could see the low-voiced conversation taking place. 'What's the matter?' he roared. 'What's the hold-up?'

Miss O'Donovan turned back into the room to explain. Sandy went with her. Galland listened and looked at Sandy.

'Why d'you want to be first?' he asked.

'It's not that I particularly want to be first, sir. It's just that I find the corridor awfully draughty. Perhaps you could take us both at the same time, could you?'

Sir Vian put on his glasses and pursed his lips. 'I have no objections,' he said. 'Have you, gentlemen?'

'Not me,' said Dr Galland.

'No, no, anything to get it finished with,' the Superintendent said testily.

Sir Vian took off his glasses again and began to polish them with a pink silicone tissue. He had a supply of these in front of him on the table and in fact was famous for this trait, which had earned him the name of Polishing Partick. He looked kindly at Erica.

'Well now, Staff Nurse, as you know we've been told that it was after a conversation with you that Dr Dugall absented himself. We'd like to hear, in your own words, what took place.'

'Yes, sir.' Erica cleared her throat. 'Well, Dr Dugall had left the dining hall because of what was said in the revue——'

'Yes, yes,' muttered Sir Vian, polishing hard. 'I was there. Very unkind, very uncalled-for.'

'Tell us what Dr Dugall said to you,' Dr Matthewes commanded. 'And also what you said to Dr Dugall.'

'Staff Nurse Ryall really said very little,' Sandy told him. 'The main part of the conversation was between Dr Dugall and myself.'

'Indeed? Could you give us an account of that, Dr Legrady?'

'Certainly. I told Dugall he was silly to be upset by the nonsense in the revue. In fact I lost my temper with him. It was because of a tactless remark of mine that Dr Dugall walked out.'

'Could you tell us what you said?'

Sandy coloured a little. 'I told him to snap out of his moodiness and self-pity. I've since realised that Dr Dugall was going through a phase of basic insecurity about his choice of career, so my remarks must have seemed very ill-judged to him.'

Dr Matthewes pounced on part of this information.

'Basic insecurity? Pardon me, this is entirely new ground to me. Do I understand that Dr Dugall had troubles of that sort?'

'Unfortunately, yes. He was unable to confide his private troubles to anyone except Nurse Ryall, who could tell you a great deal that would be very helpful. I myself found out what she knew, but it's only fairly recently I've done what I should have done all along—that's to say, try to get to know my junior colleague and give him reassurance.'

'Staff Nurse, can you shed any light on this?'

Erica didn't know what to do. 'Oh well—you see, Sir Vian, what Dr Dugall said to me was in confidence——'

Sandy interrupted by laying a hand on her arm. 'Please, Erica,' he said in a low voice. 'I think you ought to tell.'

Since he wanted it—and since she trusted him—Erica told them the reason for Ian's doubts. She spoke simply and briefly, but somehow conveyed the immense problem with which Ian had been grappling alone.

'The harder he tried,' she ended, 'the more tense and worried he grew. The more tense he was, the less he felt in contact with his patients. He felt he had no real calling to the work.'

'But I think he was wrong,' Sandy took it up. 'And he knows it now. I was Dr Dugall's patient myself a few days ago, as you know, and I can tell you that a more devoted or dedicated man doesn't exist. He was wrong to leave the hospital without permission as he did, and I think he himself would be the first to agree to that. But indirectly I think it's been a good thing because it's given him a chance to learn what he couldn't have found out any other way. He's a born doctor.'

'I see,' Dr Matthewes said thoughtfully. 'I see. Dr

Galland, you told me you thought Dugall had coped remarkably well up at that farmhouse all on his own?'

'I do think so. Mind you, I think some of the credit should go to Staff Nurse Ryall,' he added, glaring round the table as if daring them to argue. 'And I think we ought to analyse the concoction Dr Dugall unearthed at Coult's shack—it may have useful therapeutic qualities even though it is a folk-remedy.'

The others murmured agreement. A moment later Erica was told she could go. Almost immediately after, Sandy came out. He dropped rather wearily on the chair next to Ian.

'I think you're all right,' he told him. 'They'll call you in a minute to let you know their decision. If it's a gentle smack on the wrist, as I imagine it will be, don't be ashamed to let them know how relieved and pleased you are. They want to be assured that you're the right stuff— and as you are, you may as well let them know it!'

Ian was called in. He was gone for quite a while. They could just hear Dr Matthewes' voice going on and on, but they couldn't distinguish the words. It sounded like a re-proving lecture.

And then Ian was closing the door behind him, and wiping his brow, and then dancing round the room waving his hands over his head.

' "Nervous strain"!' he crowed. ' "Don't let it happen again"! Oh, gosh, oh, gee, I feel like the first man in space!'

His demonstration was cut short as the committee members began to come out. They gave him a smiling nod as they passed.

'Congratulations, Ian,' Erica said with sincere gladness. 'From now on everything's going to be all right, isn't it?'

'From now on,' said Ian, 'I've got problems. Do you

realise I'm due to leave Reidmouth in six weeks and I haven't even begun applying for house-surgeon vacancies?'

'Have you any idea whereabouts you'd like to go?'

'None at all. If there were any vacancies coming up here I'd try to stay on at Reidmouth. You see, I was so sure I'd be giving up medicine that I didn't even bother to look at the advertised posts.'

'I believe there's one going at Fordingham—it's rather nice there, you can get in to Christchurch quite easily.'

'You were there?'

'Yes, at one stage in my career.'

'I suppose you wouldn't care to give me a hand drafting my application?'

'When? This evening? I'm going home for a few days tomorrow.'

'In that case, I wouldn't dream of asking——'

'No, it's quite all right. I'd be glad to help. If we could do it fairly early in the evening? I've some packing to attend to, and I'd rather like an early night.'

'That would suit me fine. Then I could take my mother out afterwards to a little celebration dinner. Oh, great Scott!' he added. 'My poor mother! She's sitting in that hotel waiting to hear the verdict. I must rush off to her immediately if not sooner.'

'Before you rush off—what about your farewell party?'

'A party?'

'Yes, like the one you came to, your first day at Reidmouth. That was to say goodbye to Bobby Guest—remember Bobby, Erica? We'll have to give you a party, Ian. We'll choose a date this evening.'

'Right you are. Erica, are you doing anything this evening? You wouldn't like to come to dinner?'

'Oh, I'm sure your mother would like to have you to herself tonight, Ian.'

'Oh—well, perhaps that's true. Tomorrow, then? No, hang it, tomorrow I'm back on duty. Oh, do say you'll come!'

She agreed smilingly, and Ian rushed away. Sandy watched him taking the drive at an energetic sprint, and nodded approvingly.

'That's better,' he said. 'That's the way he *should* be.'

'It's thanks to you, mainly.' She turned rather worried eyes upon him. 'You look tired, Sandy. A few days at home will do you the world of good.'

'I suppose you wouldn't be free to come and see me off tomorrow?'

'I'm on duty, I'm afraid.'

'I was afraid of that. Well,' he said, jokingly, but with an underlying sadness, 'don't forget me when I'm gone, will you?'

There was no danger of that. She thought of him often, and spoke of him too—to Ian, who would once have kindled to anger at the mere mention of his name. But that was all in the past, as was the façade of self-importance that had once hidden the real Ian Dugall. It was too late now to begin making any lasting friendships at Reidmouth, but Ian was at least accepted by most people. Erica was spared the agony of having to refuse invitations because Ian hadn't been included; they went out together in a group, the younger members of the medical staff and the unmarried men who wanted to join them, with an appropriate number of girl-friends. And when Sandy came back from his home on the fruit farm beyond Nelson, he too joined the happy band.

Ian wrote out his applications and sent them off. To his great satisfaction, he obtained the post that Sandy had originally recommended, that of house-surgeon at Fordingham.

The day of his farewell party, Erica found herself going through her preparations with the same unhelpful comments from Marion as on a previous occasion. This seemed unjust, for Marion was going to the party too with Tom Quillan; so logically she ought to have been too busy with her own preparations to bother Erica. However, Ian had asked to call for Erica at a surprisingly early hour, and so she was putting on her lipstick and doing her hair a full half hour before Marion need start.

'I see you've got another new dress,' Marion commented. 'For whose benefit? Ian or Sandy?'

'Don't talk nonsense,' said Erica, laughing, and picked up her coat from the bed.

Ian was waiting downstairs. He took her by the elbow and ushered her out, and now at last she discovered the reason for their early rendezvous. Outside, by the kerb, stood a neat little saloon car—not new, but in good condition.

'Do you like it?' he asked eagerly. 'Come on, I'll show you how nicely it runs. We've got plenty of time for a spin along towards Glenfalloch.'

She had to agree it was a smooth-running car. And that the heater worked. And the radio.

'You'll find it useful in Fordingham,' she commented. 'You'll be able to get up to Christchurch on your day off, if you want to.'

'I thought it might come in useful for more than that,' he replied. 'I could come to Reidmouth on my free week-end to see you.'

'Fordingham to Reidmouth—that's a long trip.'

'I wouldn't mind. If I felt you wanted me to come, Erica, I'd be here at every opportunity.'

Uncertain what to say, she turned her head and looked out of the window. As they drove by, she could see that the rata trees were showing flower buds which would soon

182

burst into scarlet blossom; it seemed such a short time ago that she had watched with regret as last year's blossoms fluttered to the ground.

He pulled up in a turning close to Upper Harbour, and they sat in silence for a while.

'Do you want me to come and see you, Erica?'

'I—I'd always be glad to see you, Ian.' She turned back to meet his gaze.

'Glad? Not more than that?' He reached for her hand. 'Erica, what am I going to do when I leave here? How shall I manage without you?'

'You'll be all right, Ian. Your problems are behind you.'

'I needn't be without you, Erica—if you'll come and join me in Fordingham.'

She studied him earnestly. Then she gave a gentle shake of the head. 'We're not in love, you know, Ian.'

'You're wrong, Erica. I love you——'

'Yes, perhaps you do—and I love you too, with an affection that I know will never alter. But we're not in love. Once you get to Fordingham you'll become immersed in your work and begin to make friends there. And my importance will seem less and less every day. I hope you'll always think of me with fondness, but you'll find you can live without me.'

'No, darling, I can't. I dread the thought of life without you——'

'But you'll survive, all the same. My dear, I'm just the girl who was able to give you sympathy and companionship when you needed it.'

'Sympathy and companionship? Is that all? Then what did it mean when you told Sandy I was the most important thing in the world?'

'That's not exactly what I said. I said finding you was the most important thing in the world—and so it was. If I hadn't succeeded in that, I'd still be regretting it at this moment. But I'm not in love with you. I never pretended I was. And you're not in love with me, though you may think you are. You'll see. A year from now you'll be glad it all passed off quietly.'

'But I want you to marry me!'

She pressed his hand and then freed her own. 'I could say to you, "Ask me again in a year's time," because I know in a year's time you won't want to. But instead I'll say, quite simply, "No, I won't marry you, dearest Ian" and leave you free instead of worrying about having to ask me next year!'

'You're laughing at me,' he said ruefully.

'Never in this world. I'm too fond of you to laugh at you. I'd like to think of myself as the girl whose name is at the top of your list of friends—a list that I know will be a long one by and by. But one day you'll meet a girl, and she'll be someone special, not just someone to add to your list of friends.'

'Think it over, Erica,' he begged. 'Think it over for a few days and write to me at Fordingham.'

'I'll write to you. But I shan't think it over. While I'm face to face with you now I know I'm not in love with you, although I value your friendship more than anything else that's come my way.'

He smiled a little. 'Well, that's something,' he said. He slipped his arm round her and kissed her gently. 'That was a goodbye kiss,' he said, 'goodbye to all my hopes and plans.'

'But you'll make others,' she said softly.

They left the car in the lane and walked the short distance to Sandy's flat. The party seemed to be making a lively debut; music and laughter drifted from the open windows. They went up the wooden staircase and rang the bell.

Sandy let them in. Erica thought he studied them both with keenness, but he said a brief welcome and sent them in to join the throng.

By about eleven o'clock the party had reached the stage where it was bowling along of its own momentum. Dancing was in full swing. Ian had been cornered by the wife of one of the Junior Registrars and was being taught the latest version of the Watusi. Erica, glad of the chance to find a little peace and quiet, slipped out for a breath of fresh air.

She tiptoed down the wooden stairs. It was a night of stars, whose reflections danced in the dark waters of the harbour. At first the cold air was delightful, but after a few minutes she shivered and wished she had brought a coat.

As if in answer to the wish, her coat was placed round her shoulders. She wheeled, to find Sandy at her elbow.

'You shouldn't be out without a wrap,' he said. 'You'll catch cold.'

'I suppose I was silly. But it seemed so tempting, just to slip away from the noise and the stuffiness.'

He nodded agreement. 'I don't know why it is,' he remarked, taking her by the arm and strolling with her down the quay, 'but medical personnel below the rank of consultant seem to get a trifle rowdy, and above the rank of consultant they get solemn and confidential. Have you noticed this phenomenon?'

'I can't say I have,' she laughed. 'But then I don't go to many parties that consultants attend.'

'This one's turning out well. Before it got under way, I half expected it to turn out an engagement party.'

'An engagement party?'

She drew to a standstill and moving apart from him a little, gazed out over the harbour. 'He asked me,' she told him without looking round. 'I said no.'

'You don't love him?'

'Not the way I'd want to love the man I marry.'

'That's what I thought,' he said quietly. 'But I wasn't sure you were aware of it. I thought you'd very likely say yes. You did once tell me he was tremendously important to you.'

'I told you it was tremendously important to discover his whereabouts—which is quite a different thing.'

'Is that what you said? I wish my memory hadn't played me false, then. It's given me the most miserable few weeks of my life. I really thought—I thought you'd marry him.'

The unsteadiness of his voice told her what he'd gone through. She said, hardly knowing she said it, 'Oh, darling— you needn't have been afraid——'

'Erica!'

He caught the hand she held out. He drew her near, and his arm slipped around her. She was still only half aware of what she had said. All she knew was that suddenly a tumultuous pounding of her heart told her that she was in love. Happiness engulfed her like a tidal wave.

She confided her whole heart to him with her eager response to his kisses. She wanted him to know how deeply she loved him, she wanted him to know because it would make him happy—and to give happiness to Sandy was the most important thing in the world. In return she received from him an enchantment of the senses that seemed to heighten every feeling. The caress of his hand upon her hair, the hard strength of his arms around her, his lips pressing against hers—each sensation was distinct and yet merged into an ecstatic dream.

'Erica—my darling—I can hardly believe it!' He murmured the words softly. 'There have been times when I've almost given up hope that you'd learn to care for me.'

'I learned,' she whispered. 'I learned the hard way. Oh, Sandy, if I could tell you——! That time up at

Heights Pass, when there was a real chance that I might lose you——! And it would have been all my fault—my fault from beginning to end.'

'Do you want me to lose my temper with you?' he said with pretended sternness. 'I shall, you know, if you talk such nonsense.'

'I'm not afraid of you. I shall say what I like—and it's not nonsense, anyhow. I tell you, Sandy, when I think how I might have cost you your life, I get a nightmarish feeling that makes me want to run away and hide.'

'Don't do that. At least, don't hide where I can't find you. Because I love you so much, Erica, that my life would be empty without you. You know that, though.'

'Yes,' she agreed in a whisper, 'I know, because it's how I feel about you.'

He kept one arm round her as they wandered on down the quay, stopping now and then to exchange a fleeting kiss. By and by they reached the edge of the harbour, from which the sea rolled out towards the horizon.

'If we walk any further,' he remarked dreamily, 'we shall fall in the ocean and get wet. So I suppose we'd better turn about and go back. After all, I *am* the host at that party back there.'

'Oh yes,' she said, remembering it, 'the party.'

'Shall we tell them? About us?'

'Not yet, dearest. Let's keep it to ourselves a while. Besides——'

'Ian?'

She nodded.

'Yes, it's best to let him go to his new job and find fresh interests, before we break the news.'

'And as you once said, we've got all the time in the world ahead of us. Just think of it, Sandy—the rest of our lives!'

'All the time in the world,' he agreed. 'And all the happiness.'

<u>Two</u> more Doctor Nurse Romances to look out for this month

Mills & Boon Doctor Nurse Romances are proving very popular indeed. So from this July on, we publish an extra story each month. Stories will range wide throughout the world of medicine — from high-technology modern hospitals to the lonely life of a nurse in a small rural community. These are the other two titles for July.

ALL FOR CAROLINE
by Sarah Franklin

Megan Lacey takes up the job of speech therapist simply as a way of avenging her cousin's broken heart. But she makes a complete mess of things — and loses her own heart into the bargain.

THE SISTER AND THE SURGEON
by Lynne Collins

Sister Ruth Challis is amazed to find her cold heart melting towards untrustworthy consultant, Oliver Manning, but complications increase when her old friend Daniel's feelings about her become significant . . .

On sale where you buy Mills & Boon romances.

The Mills & Boon rose is the rose of romance

Masquerade
Historical Romances

Intrigue
excitement
romance

THE EAGLE'S FATE
by Dinah Dean

When Napoleon invaded Russia, Nadya had to walk from Moscow with her possessions on her back. She expected pity from Captain Andrei Valyev, but he seemed to hate her — why, then, had he rescued her from a fate worse than death?

MAN WITH A FALCON
by Caroline Martin

Richenda rather welcomed the excitement when the Civil War came to the very gates of her home, Black Castle. But that was before she had encountered the Royalist leader, Sebastian, Lord Devenish!

Look out for these titles in your local paperback shop from
10th July 1981

Look out for these three great Doctor Nurse Romances coming next month

CHATEAU NURSE
by Jan Haye

After an attack of pneumonia, Nurse Hilary Hope jumps at the chance of doing some private nursing in France but does not expect her life to be turned upside down by the local devastating doctor there, Raoul de la Rue ...

HOSPITAL IN THE MOUNTAINS
by Jean Evans

After a terrible car accident, Nurse Jill Sinclair accompanies her injured brother to an Austrian clinic where Baron von Reimer hopes to repair his injuries. But the Doctor Baron is such an attractive man that Jill soon finds herself in an impossible situation ...

OVER THE GREEN MASK
by Lisa Cooper

An exciting new part of her life begins when Nurse Jennifer Turner first reports at the Princess Beatrice Hospital – but nothing works out as she'd dreamed after she meets handsome registrar, Nicholas Smythe.

On sale where you buy Mills & Boon romances.

The Mills & Boon rose is the rose of romance

Doctor Nurse Romances

Have you enjoyed these recent titles in our
Doctor Nurse series?

NURSE AT SEA
by Judith Worthy .

Nurse Carole Wilson hopes a long sea voyage from
Australia to Britain will solve her emotional problems.
But when she finds the Ship's Surgeon is an old
boyfriend of hers, it is a case of out of the frying pan
into the fire ...

THE UNWILLING LOVE
by Lucy Bowdler

Janice Colby starts her first job at Nootak — as nurse
to Eskimos — and has a warm welcome from everyone
except the handsome Mountie Philip Anson, who is as
chilly as the surroundings.